MW00462245

CHOCOLATE MOUSSE ATTACK

Sally Berneathy

Books by Sally Berneathy

Death by Chocolate
(book 1 in the Death by Chocolate series)

Murder, Lies and Chocolate
(book 2 in the Death by Chocolate series)

The Great Chocolate Scam
(book 3 in the Death by Chocolate series)

Chocolate Mousse Attack
(book 4 in the Death by Chocolate series)

Fatal Chocolate Obsession
(book 5 in the Death by Chocolate series)

Deadly Chocolate Addiction
(book 6 in the Death by Chocolate series)

Guns, Wives and Chocolate
(book 7 in the Death by Chocolate series)

Spies, Lies and Chocolate Pies
(book 8 in the Death by Chocolate series)

The Ex Who Wouldn't Die
(book 1 in Charley's Ghost series)

The Ex Who Glowed in the Dark
(book 2 in Charley's Ghost series)

The Ex Who Conned a Psychic
(book 3 in Charley's Ghost series)

The Ex Who Saw a Ghost
(book 4 in Charley's Ghost series)

The Ex Who Hid a Deadly Past
(book 5 in Charley's Ghost series)

This book is a work of fiction. The names, characters, places and incidents are products of the writer's imagination or have been used fictitiously and are not to be construed as real. Any resemblance to persons, living or dead, or to actual events, locales or organizations is entirely coincidental (except for Fred and King Henry).

Chocolate Mousse Attack
Copyright ©2013 Sally Berneathy

This book may not be reproduced in whole or in part without written permission from
Sally Berneathy.
http://www.sallyberneathy.com

Original cover art by Aurora Publicity
https://www.aurorapublicity.com

<u>Chapter One</u>

Kansas City in August. People vacation in hell because it's cooler there.

The air conditioning in my kitchen at Death by Chocolate shot craps just before noon on a 102/90 day...a hundred and two degrees, ninety percent humidity. My shop is actually in Pleasant Grove, a suburb of Kansas City, but it's all the same in terms of weather. By the time I got home that afternoon my T-shirt, shorts and face were streaked with sweat and chocolate and my ponytail was a mass of red frizz.

The thought of meeting somebody new ranked way down on my wish list, somewhere between sitting in a sauna for an hour while wearing a fur coat and going on a date with my ex-husband.

When I saw Fred, my next-door neighbor, standing on the porch of the formerly vacant house across the street, talking to a woman, I hesitated, torn between curiosity and a desire to rush into my house, strip off my clothes and stand in a cold shower until the cold water ran out.

The house across the street had been vacant a lot of years except for assorted rodents and roaches and, of course, the time Paula's ex-husband hid in the attic to spy on her. But I guess that last part's redundant. He qualifies for either of the first two categories.

A couple of months ago workmen had suddenly converged on the three-story structure and launched into an extensive renovation. The jungle of trees, bushes and weeds became a sedate lawn. They painted the house a blue gray color then the fish scale siding white and the gingerbread trim maroon. The house used to remind me of an elegant, aging dowager. After the redo, it looked like a regal Victorian lady in her best ball gown.

And Fred, who was half hermit, half nerd and half mystery man (yes, I know that equals one and a half, which is a perfect description of Fred) was standing on the front porch of that house, talking to a beautiful woman, probably the new owner.

For a fleeting instant I considered giving in to curiosity, dashing over and insinuating myself into the conversation in a friendly, welcome-to-the-neighborhood sort of way. But then a gust of oven-hot wind blew a stray wisp of hair onto my cheek where it stuck. I took that as a sign.

I ducked my head and kept walking from my doddering garage toward my slightly more stable house. There's a time for curiosity and a time for hiding. Hair stuck to the cheek is a time for hiding.

I had my foot on the first step of my front porch when I heard Fred call my name. I won't say he has eyes in the back of his head because that would be silly. His hair would still get in the way. But he does have a way of seeing everything going on around him.

I peeled the bit of hair from the sweat on my face, tucked it into my pony tail, squared my shoulders and walked across the street, down the brand new sidewalk and up to the brand new wraparound porch with pristine white columns.

The afternoon sun glinted off the lenses of Fred's black framed glasses as he turned to me. I preferred his old wire frames but he listened to my opinion about as often as my cat did. "Lindsay Powell, this is our new neighbor, Sophie Fleming."

Sophie smiled, teeth white and sparkling against olive skin, and extended a slender, well-manicured hand. She was beautiful, even up close. She had flawless skin and a smooth curtain of long dark hair with no sign of frizz even in the heat and humidity. Although she'd obviously been unpacking, her beige shirt and khaki shorts looked fresh and barely rumpled. I, of course, had dirt, grease and lots of chocolate on my sweaty T-shirt and cutoffs. Standing next to Sophie, I felt even grungier than a few minutes before.

I accepted her hand. Cool and dry. Of course it was. "Welcome to the neighborhood." I smiled, hoping I didn't have spinach stuck in my teeth. I hadn't eaten any spinach that day, but Sophie's perfection made me worry that I might have it in my teeth anyway. "Place looks great."

"Thank you." She glanced back at the house. "This has been a labor of love. My parents and I lived here when I was a little girl before..." She hesitated for a brief instant, and it seemed a cloud passed between the sun and her face. Of course it didn't. Not in August. "Before we moved to Nebraska," she

3

continued. "It broke my heart to find it had become so rundown."

We knew all that, of course, thanks to Fred's prowess on the Internet. Well, we knew she and her family moved to Nebraska when she was five. We didn't know why that cloud came over her face when she talked about it. Assuming there really was a cloud. Maybe I was just looking for some slight imperfection in my new neighbor so I wouldn't have to hate her.

"We're very glad you've returned," Fred said.

Dirty old man.

"Yes, we are." I really was. I liked her instinctively in spite her being gorgeous and having straight hair and enough money to restore the house to showplace condition and not sweating in the heat.

"As soon as I get everything unpacked and set up, I'd love to have both of you over for dinner and a tour of the place, if you'd like."

"We'd like! Fred will bring wine because he's a connoisseur and I'll bring dessert because I'm chocolatier."

She beamed. "Wonderful."

Fred and I left her to enjoy her new home.

"She seems nice," I said as we strolled across the street.

"Yes, she does."

"You like her."

He frowned. "Of course I like her. She's done nothing to merit my dislike. I even like you in spite of the number of things you've done to merit my dislike."

I shot him a scowl. "Name one thing I've done that my chocolate doesn't compensate for."

"Did you bring home anything?"

"Chocolate chip cookies. Your favorite."

"I'm making spaghetti with homemade pasta and garlic bread. It should be ready in about two hours."

"I'll be there with chocolate on and sweat off."

I went to my house and Fred went to his.

King Henry, the cat who adopted me a couple of years ago, ran to greet me as soon as I opened the front door. He rubbed against my leg and looked up with big blue eyes. He didn't care if I was stinky and sweaty. Fred loves me for my chocolate and Henry loves me for my can opener. It's good to be loved.

∝∾⊰

I slept really soundly that night. Meeting Sophie and knowing she was living in what used to be a creepy old house somehow made the neighborhood feel safer. Being in an air conditioned bedroom after the heated kitchen probably helped too.

When the sound of *Wild Bull Rider* pulled me from a deep sleep, I sat bolt upright in bed, heart pounding, and grabbed for my phone. *Wild Bull Rider* is Fred's ringtone. I don't know that he's ever ridden any wild bulls, but I don't know that he hasn't.

One thing I did know, he never called after ten o'clock at night or before nine in the morning, and my clock clearly said two a.m. No good news ever comes at two in the morning.

A thousand possibilities, none of them good, flitted through my mind in the seconds it took to grab the phone and accept the call.

Aliens had come to take Fred back to his home planet and he was calling to say good-bye.

A burglar had broken into his house, stolen his phone and was pocket-dialing me.

Fred had awakened with a sudden craving for brownies.

All that was ridiculous, of course, but nothing compared to the reality.

"Lindsay, I need you to come over here." As always his voice was firm, his words precise, but I detected an edge of panic.

"Are you all right? Are you hurt? Have you fallen and can't get up?" Fred wasn't young, but he wasn't old either. He'd always seemed ageless and invulnerable. The thought that he might be hurt and need my help clenched my heart into a cold, painful knot.

"Do you remember Sophie Fleming, the woman who moved into the house across the street?"

"Did you call me at two a.m. just to test my memory? Yes, I remember her. Tall brunette with hair down to her butt and no perspiration on her brow. Can I go back to sleep now?"

"No. I told you I need you here. Sophie Fleming won't come out of my closet."

It's often difficult to tell if Fred's being funny or serious. His expression and tone rarely change. I couldn't see his expression at that moment, and his tone was calm but with just a hint of desperation. I decided to play it straight.

"Why is Sophie Fleming in your closet?"

"If I knew the answer to that question, I wouldn't be calling you."

"Which closet is she in?" I didn't suppose it made a lot of difference, but I was trying to get a picture of what the heck was going on at Fred's house.

"My bedroom closet."

"Is this some kind of kinky sex thing?"

"Lindsay, if you ever again want me to help you break into somebody's house or hack into a website illegally or get a speeding ticket erased from the system, you need to stop asking stupid questions and get over here now." He hung up.

That was the closest I'd ever known Fred to get to all-out panic mode. He's more than capable of dragging one or more people out of his closet and tossing them on their butt in the street, but a beautiful woman apparently had him completely freaked out.

I swung my feet out of bed and onto the hardwood floor. Henry, sleeping off a catnip binge on the foot of my bed, lifted his head, opened one blue eye and gave a questioning meow but was back asleep before I could answer. Good thing. I didn't relish trying to explain something to him that I didn't understand.

I sleep in an old T-shirt patterned with the M&M guys. It's big and comfortable and would do for a night time visit. I grabbed a pair of shorts and pulled them on then hurried downstairs, making a quick detour through the kitchen to grab a Coke and a plastic container of chocolate chip cookies. I needed the Coke, and it sounded like Fred might need the cookies.

As I crossed Fred's yard where every blade of grass is always three inches long and the flowers never have wilted blooms, I took a moment to look for the elves I'm sure do his yard work in the middle of the night. I thought I caught a glimpse of one skulking in a car parked in front of my house, but everybody knows there's no such thing as elves in the Kansas City area. It gets too cold in the winter. Probably just my scuzzy ex-husband stalking me. He does that when he's in between bimbos.

The street was lined with mature trees and the car was parked in the shadows, as far away from streetlights as he could get. Nevertheless I was pretty sure the elf's hair was blond. Definitely Rick though the car wasn't familiar. A mid-size white sedan. Not his style but it could belong to a new bimbo. I considered going over to confront him and yell at him for a while, but Fred's crisis was more important than a moment's pleasure.

Fred met me at his front door. His immaculate white hair was mussed, his glasses were slightly askew, and he wore white cotton pajamas that were somehow unwrinkled despite the hour. He looked more like he'd come from a Karate workout than the bedroom.

"Please tell me you didn't iron those pajamas," I said by way of greeting.

He glared at me. Yes, Fred actually glared at me. That was a lot of emotion for him to display.

Then his gaze dropped to my hands. "Are those cookies for me?"

I handed him the container.

"Thank you." He turned and I followed him into his immaculate home.

Like his yard, his house is always immaculate. His hardwood floors are always shiny and no speck of dust mars his furniture. Elves again. They come in the middle of the night to clean, then they dump his dust in my house.

"Do you want to tell me how Sophie Fleming got into your bedroom closet in the first place?" I asked as we started up the stairs.

"She walked in there. Actually, it was closer to a run. Speed walk, to be specific."

He strode onto the landing and down the hall toward his bedroom, his long strides longer than usual and his steps hurried. That was as stressed as I'd ever seen Fred. Things were getting a little freaky.

I got another shock when I entered his bedroom. The covers on one side of the bed were thrown back. Sure, the average person wouldn't make his bed when he got up in the middle of the night to try to lure a strange woman out of his closet, but Fred wasn't the average person. Anyway, he had those elves.

He strode to the open closet door and I followed.

The closet was large for an old house. On one side shirts were grouped by color, fabric and long sleeves versus short sleeves. On the other, slacks and jackets were arranged the same way. He had a shoe rack which held polished shoes and a tie rack with ties, sorted by color, of course. Sophie huddled in one corner at the very back, face between her knees, dark curtain of hair flowing over her arms where they wrapped protectively around her head, white lacy gown spreading about her.

A beautiful woman in a night gown hiding in the bedroom closet of a man in pajamas. If it had been anybody but Fred...

"Sophie?" I spoke softly.

She flinched and tightened her arms around her head.

I turned to Fred. "How did she get in your house? I feel certain you have the door locked."

He straightened his glasses. "At 1:33 a.m. my security system told me someone was on my front porch. I went down to investigate and saw her trying to get in. I opened the door and asked if I could be of assistance. She walked past me, straight up the stairs and into my bedroom closet. I believe she's sleep-walking, but I can't seem to wake her or persuade her to come out." He removed a cookie from the container and bit into it. His hand shook slightly. I was glad I had brought the cookies. He needed a fix.

I took the container from him. Maybe Sophie would respond to a cookie. Chocolate has restorative powers.

I handed Fred my Coke and moved into the closet where I knelt next to her, pushing Fred's pants aside. "Sophie, it's Lindsay. I'm your neighbor. Remember me? Chocolatier?"

She shivered but didn't look up.

"Would you like a chocolate chip cookie? I made them myself."

Nothing.

There's something very wrong with anyone who turns down one of my cookies.

I touched her arm.

Her head flew up and she shoved my hand away. Her eyes were wide and filled with terror. "Carolyn! No!"

I had a bad feeling it was going to take more than a few cookies to help that woman.

<u>Chapter Two</u>

"Who's Carolyn?" The question came out of my mouth automatically. I didn't really expect a response, but Sophie blinked a couple of times and awareness came back to her eyes.

"Carolyn?" she repeated. Her gaze darted from side to side, from shirts to pants and back again. "Where...? What...?" Eyes wide, she scrambled to her feet.

"It's okay." I hung onto a pair of gray slacks as I got up to stand beside her. "It's me, Lindsay, your new neighbor. Remember?"

She looked at me, her expression wild and confused. "Yes, Lindsay, I remember. Where am I? How did I get here? What's going on?"

Fred stepped inside the closet. "We were hoping you could tell us."

She gasped at the sight of Fred and clutched my arm convulsively. He doesn't usually have that effect on women.

"I told you not to get those black framed glasses," I said. Never pass up a chance to say *I told you so*.

Sophie relaxed her grip. "You're Fred Sommers. You live across the street. I..." She looked around her again, studying the categorized clothing, then swallowed audibly. "Is this your house?"

"Yes. Would you like to come out of the closet and sit down?"

"I have cookies." I held out the container. Whatever the circumstances, offer food or beverage. My mother taught me manners.

"I..."

Fred held out his hand.

She looked at it doubtfully.

He stepped back from the closet. "If you'd like to go downstairs, I'll make some coffee and we can discuss this."

She shivered and looked down at her gown. "I've been sleepwalking again." Her voice was quiet, without emotion, resigned.

Sleepwalking was a little weird, but I supposed it was better than having a neighbor who was psycho.

"I'll get you a robe and then we'll go downstairs and have coffee and some of Lindsay's cookies."

He disappeared and she looked at me. "I'm sorry. This hasn't happened since I was a child."

I shrugged. "The stress of moving, meeting new people. Don't worry about it. Fred needs a little excitement in his life. Nobody's tried to kill him in a couple of months."

Before she could ask what I meant, Fred returned with a white terry cloth robe and handed it to Sophie.

We went downstairs to the breakfast nook. The large bay window looked out on a wonderful view of trees whose leaves disappeared into thin air before they could fall to the ground and birds that never pooped. Of course it was dark so we couldn't see all that, but I could feel the tidiness pressing against the window, trying to get inside and attack me.

While Fred made coffee, Sophie and I sat at the polished oak table that absorbed crumbs before they had a chance to settle on its surface.

"This isn't necessary," Sophie said. "I should go home. I've disturbed you all enough already."

"It's okay, really. I get up at four anyway to go to work, and I'm not sure Fred ever sleeps. I think he's part robot."

"I'm standing right here. I can hear you talking about me." Fred set two cups of coffee and a fresh Coke on the table then took a chair across from Sophie.

I picked up the Coke. "The robot theory explains the super hearing."

Sophie wrapped her hands around the mug Fred had set in front of her. "I'm so sorry I woke you two."

"Who's Carolyn?" Fred asked.

A beautiful woman with a mystery. Fred was hooked.

And I was mildly curious.

Sophie frowned. "I don't know anyone named Carolyn. Why do you keep asking me about that name?"

I took a sip of Coke and studied her. She seemed genuinely puzzled. "When I tried to wake you, you called me that name."

"I did?" She shook her head. "It's a common name. I've probably known a Carolyn somewhere over the years."

14

"Do you remember what you were dreaming?" Fred asked.

"Yes." She bit her lip and her forehead furrowed. "It was scary. There was a man with a knife and...blood." She gave a slight shrug and attempted an even slighter smile. "A nightmare."

"It's unlikely a man is going to be named Carolyn," I said. "Was there a woman in your dream?"

"No."

Her answer came so quickly I didn't quite believe her.

She toyed with her cup, studying the dark liquid as if it were a crystal ball where she could find answers. She hadn't taken even a sip. I'm a Coke and tea person myself, but I was certain Fred made good coffee no matter how oxymoronic that term sounded to me.

"So you had problems with sleepwalking when you were a child?" Fred asked.

She looked up and shrugged. "It's pretty typical for kids, I guess. I grew out of it."

"When you lived across the street as a child, did you know the people in this house, maybe come over to visit sometimes?"

Sophie bit her lip. "I don't think so. I don't remember who lived here. I believe the place was vacant. I was very young when we moved away."

"But you remembered living here. You wanted to come back to your old house."

She gave a tight smile. "My parents died not long after we moved to Nebraska. My memories of living here are..." She spread her hands as if

15

searching for the right words. "I have only vague memories of childhood, memories of a happy home with my parents. My aunt, my mother's sister who raised me, was wonderful, but I never forgot my mother and father. When I decided to start my own interior decorating company and discovered my old house was for sale, it seemed like a sign. So I made the decision to move here." She rose stiffly. "I do apologize. I promise to lock myself inside every night from here on out so this won't happen again."

Fred stood also. "No problem. I was going to ask you over for coffee anyway." He smiled.

Sophie relaxed noticeably, her own smile becoming more genuine and less forced. "I'll bring your robe back tomorrow."

Fred walked her to the door, and he and I stood on his porch until she was safely inside her house.

"Well," I said, "that was strange. Remember when people kept trying to get in my basement to get the money that wasn't there? Maybe there's hidden treasure in your house and she came over to find it. Maybe she wasn't really sleepwalking. Maybe somebody buried gold here and she needs to find it to pay for all the renovations on that house."

Fred sighed and shook his head. "You have quite an imagination."

❦

I didn't see any point in going back to bed so I dressed and went in to work early. By the time Paula got there, I'd already made up a batch of chocolate chip cookie dough and eaten a substantial part of it. After a hard night of hauling strange women out of the closet, there's nothing like a breakfast of cookie dough and Coke.

"Come in early to take advantage of the cooler morning?" she asked as she tied on a heavy apron.

I pulled out a mixing bowl to start a Triple Chocolate Mousse Cake. "Repair guy should be here by nine. We can survive until then. No, I'm up early because Fred had a woman in his closet and couldn't get her out."

Paula paused with one hand holding her blond hair back and the other positioned to secure it with an elastic band. Her forehead creased in a frown. "Is this one of those strange euphemisms men are always coming up with?"

"No." I broke bittersweet chocolate into small pieces in a bowl and told Paula about the night's events.

She took out the dough she'd left to rise overnight in the refrigerator and began preparing cinnamon rolls. They're not chocolate, but they're pretty darn good. Extra cinnamon, extra butter. Our customers love them and I even sneak a few bites from time to time when nobody's looking. I don't want word to get out that I'm eating something other than chocolate. I have a reputation to uphold.

"Sleepwalking is more common than you might think," Paula said, "especially when the person's under stress. I'm sure our new neighbor will be fine. But you might want to remember to lock your doors at night, just in case."

Paula's always the voice of reason. The only time I've ever seen her get upset was when her psycho ex-husband kidnapped her son Zach. He's in prison now. The ex-husband, not Zach. He lives with his mother next door to me. I'm his "Anlinny." That's kid-speak for Aunt Lindsay. He can say my name now since he's all of three years old, but he still calls me Anlinny.

I put chocolate and butter into the microwave to melt. "I think I saw Rick parked in the street last night, watching my house."

Paula smacked the dough with a rolling pin bigger than her arm. "That doesn't surprise me. Rick's not the type to give up just because you have papers saying you're divorced. That man is seriously nuts."

"Your ex is seriously nuts. Mine's just crazy nuts. Rick would never try to kill me like yours did." I stirred the melted chocolate and thought about that for a minute. "But I would not be willing to sign a notarized statement to that effect."

The air conditioning guys came to fix the air conditioning, my Triple Chocolate Mousse Cake came out perfect, and I made a lot of people happy and full. It was a good day.

Near closing time, I was cleaning off tables when I looked up to see Paula standing at the counter, talking to the only guy left in the place. She talks to people all the time, taking orders, asking if they need anything else, but she actually seemed to be having a conversation with this guy.

Paula has a lot of scars—physical and emotional—from her marriage to Zach's father, and she doesn't make friends readily. It took me almost a year, working with her every day, to convince her to discuss more than the menu and how much flour we needed to order.

But she looked relaxed and was actually smiling while talking to this guy.

I couldn't tell a lot about him from his back. He wore a white shirt with dark slacks and he had blond hair—natural, not highlighted like Rick's. I moved closer to the counter, trying to get a better look and be unobtrusive while carrying a tray of dirty dishes to the kitchen. The smears on his plate indicated he'd had a piece of my Triple Chocolate Mousse Cake and had eaten every bite. That was a good sign.

I angled through the opening on the other side of the cash register and leaned around to study his face. Damn dishes leaned too. Slid right off the tray and crashed to the floor. I got a good look at the guy's face when he and Paula both jerked their heads in my direction. My initial impression of him was that he looked startled.

Paula rushed over. "Let me help you."

While we were picking up broken glass and greasy food, the bell over the door jingled. I flinched and almost cut my finger on a piece of chocolate covered glass. I hoped it wasn't the sound of Paula's guy leaving.

I stood and looked around. The stool where he'd been sitting was empty. *Way to go, Lindsay! Paula finally shows a little interest in a man, and you run him off!*

"I'm sorry," I said.

Paula put the last of the big pieces back on the tray. "Don't worry about it. I've dropped more dishes than you have." She disappeared into the kitchen and came back with a broom.

"No, I mean because your friend left when I created the big bang." I stood with the tray of broken glass and garbage.

"He wasn't my friend. I've never met him before." She swept energetically at the mess. A bit too energetically?

"But he might have become your friend if I hadn't interrupted."

Her blue-gray eyes were clear and guileless, but her cheeks had a tinge of pink. A blush? From Paula? "He was a customer. I was being polite. That's all."

I looked toward the empty stool and noticed a business card lying beside the plate. Aha! He'd left her a way to reach him!

I hurried toward the kitchen to dump my mess then come back and grab the card before Paula had a chance to throw it away without even reading it.

The bell jingled again and I turned back to look, hoping he'd returned.

It was Rick.

"We're closed." I went on to the kitchen and tossed the mess into the garbage can.

Paula followed me with the contents of her dust pan. "He just sat down at the counter."

"Of course he did." I grabbed a mop, filled a bucket with water and cleanser then returned to the front.

Rick was sitting on a stool next to the dirty dish, holding the business card. "A history professor? Are you branching out from cops to men with brains?"

I snatched the card from him and stuck it in the pocket of my cutoffs. "I'm going to take some classes. Not that it's any of your business." I ignored the remark about *cops*. Now that Rick and I were divorced, I was dating Detective Adam Trent of the Pleasant Grove Police Department. Actually we'd been sort of dating for over a year while those papers were pending, but he refused to be the official man in my life until I was officially unmarried. He's burdened with a lot of high moral standards that drive me freaking crazy sometimes. Not only did he make me wait all that time, but he refuses to fix any of my speeding tickets. Sometimes people carry those moral standards a little too far.

Since Rick had dated Muffy, Becky, Vanessa, Lisa, Susan, Mary, Julia, etc., etc., while we were married, he certainly had no right to complain about Trent, but Rick hates to lose any of his possessions, even the ones he doesn't value.

He spread his hands and smiled the smile that sold a lot of commercial real estate to gullible buyers and a lot of Rick to gullible women. Yes, I fell for it once and married him. But I was young and dumb in those days. Now I knew if he was smiling, that meant he wanted something.

"No," he said, "I don't suppose it is any of my business." His smile turned sad. "I screwed up and lost that right, didn't I?"

"Yes." I reached into the display case, withdrew the last chocolate chip cookie and handed it to him on a napkin. "Compliments of the house. Now go. We need to lock up."

As if on cue, Paula appeared from the kitchen with the shop key in her hand and went over to stand beside the front door.

Rick accepted the cookie and smiled again but made no move to leave. I sighed and waited.

He took a bite and rolled his eyes as if in ecstasy. "You make the best chocolate chip cookies in the world."

"At least we agree on one thing." I lifted the mop and let the water drain back into the bucket. "Now I really need to lock up and clean up. Everything left in here will get mopped."

Rick smiled sadly, combining two of his most effective expressions. This was going to be big!

"I miss that sense of humor," he said.

"You mean the one you used to call warped and sick and strange? That's the sense of humor you miss?"

He laughed.

"Damn it, Rick, I'm busy, I've been up since two o'clock this morning and I'm in no mood for your garbage. You have thirty seconds to get out of here before I smack you in the face with this mop."

He blanched. If I'd threatened him with a gun he'd have laughed it off, but the thought of getting mop water on his perfect hair, perfect shirt and perfect pants terrified him.

"I need a favor, Lindsay." He cleared his throat. "And I'm willing to do a favor for you. We still have some properties to sign off on, and I'm willing to throw in a little extra."

The only things I'd asked for in the divorce were my shop, Death by Chocolate, the rental house where Paula and Zach lived and the house where I lived. Death by Chocolate brings in a decent income, but I'm not getting rich. And Rick had enough money stashed in offshore accounts to qualify as pretty close to rich. I decided it wouldn't hurt to listen to what he wanted in exchange for some of his precious money.

"How much extra?"

He shrugged. "A thousand?"

"Ten."

He lifted an eyebrow. "Thousand?"

"Yep. And I already know that much wouldn't even cause a ripple in your funds."

He drew in a deep breath. "Okay. So we have a deal?"

My chest tightened in fear. If Rick agreed to part with that much money so readily, he must want a really big favor. Murder? An alibi?

"Not until you tell me who you want me to kill. If it's your mother, we might be able to work something out."

He tried to smile again, but it got stuck halfway. "It's nothing really. You'll probably enjoy it."

Paula, waiting at the front door, key in hand, ready to close up as soon as we could get rid of Rick, caught my eye and shook her head firmly.

"What do you want that's going to be so enjoyable for me you have to pay me ten thousand dollars to enjoy it?"

"Just one little favor. I need you to babysit Rickie for a couple of weeks while Ginger and I are in Hawaii."

Chapter Three

"You want me to babysit your son? Not for all the chocolate on the planet!"

Rick looked uncomfortable. I liked that look on him. "Please? Grace just dumped him on me. She's off on a honeymoon with some creep who's only interested in her because she's getting an outrageous amount of child support from me, enough you'd think she could hire a babysitter. But, no, she dropped the little…" He stopped and compressed his lips to hold back the name he'd been about to call his son. Demon child? Brat? Unholy terror? "She left him on my front porch and drove away."

I tried unsuccessfully to keep the smile off my face. "That's your problem, not mine."

"He's your stepson!"

My chin fell straight to the floor. "Excuse me? I never met that child until a month ago and even then you said he wasn't yours until DNA proved he is! No, he is not my stepson and I'm not going to babysit him!"

Rick put on his pitiful expression. "What am I supposed to do? The tickets to Hawaii are nonrefundable."

"You have two choices. Get on Craig's List and find a babysitter or eat the tickets." I nodded to Paula, and she opened the door. "Neither of those involves me. Good-bye." I lifted the mop threateningly again.

Rick stepped back, moving in the direction of the open door. "What am I going to do if I get a babysitter off Craig's List and when Grace finds out I left her son with a stranger, she takes away my visitation rights?"

I laughed. "Off the top of my head, I'd guess you'd celebrate."

"One day, Lindsay, you'll need a favor from me, and I'll remember this."

"You will remember? Been taking your ginkgo biloba, have you?"

He turned and headed for the door but not before I saw his angry expression. Rick doesn't like not getting his way.

❧❧

I left work, got in my little red Celica and called Trent before I pulled out of the parking lot. "Have I got some stories to tell you," I said as soon as he answered the phone. Because we both work crazy hours, we sometimes can't get together until the weekends. It was only Wednesday.

"Are you driving while talking on your cell phone?" he asked. As I said, sometimes he takes the business of following the rules way too seriously.

I put on my blinker to move over a lane. The car behind me sped up so I couldn't. "I'm not going fast enough to worry about it, thanks to traffic, stoplights and jerks. Anyway, I'm on my Bluetooth, and I was sitting in the parking lot when I hit your speed dial. I can make chocolate chip cookies and talk to Paula at the same time. I really think I can handle driving home and talking to you at the same time."

The car in front of me, the one being herded down the street by a young girl with a cell phone stuck to her ear, slowed. I tensed. The traffic light ahead was still green, but if she dinked around long enough, it would eventually turn red and stay red for a long time.

The light turned yellow and she stopped.

I sighed. "I'm currently parked at a two-hour red light. Do you want to hear my stories or not?"

"I want to hear your stories. I just don't want to hear the sound of crunching metal."

The light finally turned to green, but the idiot in front of me was paying more attention to her conversation than to my need to get through that intersection before I was eligible to collect Social Security. I tapped my horn. Okay, I leaned on it.

Trent sighed. "I don't even want to know who you're honking at or why."

The girl finally noticed the green light and moved on. I made it through on yellow. "Good," I said, "because I don't want to tell you. Okay, moving on. First, I met the new owner of the house across the street and Fred called at two this morning to ask me to come over and coax her out of his closet." That diverted his attention from the subject of my driving.

I was almost finished with Sophie's story, when I crested a hill, saw a motorcycle cop with a radar gun and slammed on my brakes. The officer immediately stuck his radar gun in his belt and climbed on his bike.

"Damn! Damn, damn, damn!"

"Please tell me you're not getting another speeding ticket."

I drove past the cop, pulled docilely over to the shoulder and fumbled in my purse for my license. I knew the routine.

"Lindsay? You still there?"

The motorcycle cop, lights flashing, sped right past me, chasing another car.

I laughed. "It wasn't me! He didn't give me a ticket! He's after somebody else!"

"That's good."

"Yeah, but that means somebody was going faster than I was. That's kind of humiliating." I merged back into traffic, relieved but a little sad.

By the time I pulled into my driveway at home, I had finished Sophie's tale and the story of Rick's babysitting needs.

"Call me if you need help," Trent said. "You probably haven't heard the last of Rick and little Rickie."

"I know." I got out of the car and lifted my garage door then checked up and down the street. It wouldn't have surprised me to see Rick's car parked there or even the man himself sitting in my front porch swing. He's the top salesman at Rheims Commercial Real Estate for a reason. He is relentless and doesn't understand the word *no*.

"Cookout at my house on Saturday night," I said. "You get to meet the new neighbor who has a fondness for Fred's closet."

"Cookout? In this heat? How about I bring pizzas?"

I was tempted. I do love pizza but I also love sitting outside on summer nights. "We'll see. It's only Wednesday. We've got plenty of time to figure out the details."

We hung up and I walked across the yard to my house, enjoying the faint scent of clover and the buzz of bees as they darted among clover and various other blooms. Grass is a lot of trouble not to mention that it's boring. I prefer to let the natural process of evolution prevail in my yard. *Only the strong survive.*

Needless to say, Fred doesn't share my dedication to nature. I've caught him tossing weed killer granules onto my lawn in the middle of the night. That certainly messes with the process of evolution and gives the grass an unfair advantage. But clover and dandelions are strong. So far the grass is losing the battle in spite of Fred's foreign aid.

I opened my front door and Henry met me, launching into his usual *I love you so much, Mom, and I don't need anything from you in return but if you want to give me some food, it will show how much you love me* routine.

I poured nuggets into his German shepherd size bowl then added half a can of something disgusting and smelly.

He dug in immediately, properly appreciative of the food I'd slaved over a hot can opener to produce.

Henry appeared out of nowhere a few weeks after Rick and I separated and I moved into this place. I'd made the mistake of letting Rick spend the night and was feeling guilty, sad and desperate to get rid of him when King Henry strolled into my house

28

and my life, announced he was staying and Rick was going. I've never been able to find his previous owners and have no idea of his lifestyle before he claimed me. Perhaps he had offspring I knew nothing about. Perhaps one or more of them would show up on my doorstep one day.

"Henry," I said as I watched him gobble down the disgusting food, "we've never talked about your former life, and it doesn't really matter. We both started with clean slates as far as I'm concerned. When you came here, you'd already made the decision not to have children, but Rick's mother made that decision for him when he was fifteen and he still managed to produce Rickie. So I just want you to know, if you have some descendants out there..." I paused, thinking about having another amazing cat like Henry. Then again, the kids could take after their mother. Maybe that's why he'd left home in the first place. "If you don't want to bring your kids home to meet me, if you don't ever want to talk about them, that's okay with me. Your decision."

He continued eating. I took that as a sign he didn't want to talk about his past.

I went upstairs to take a quick shower before going to Fred's to see if he knew anything else about his nighttime visitor and to tell him my latest Rickhead story.

When I pulled off my cutoffs, I found the card that Paula's admirer had left. In all the kerfuffle of Rick's intrusion, I'd forgotten about that guy.

Matthew Graham, Associate Professor of History at a local college. Beneath his business phone, he'd handwritten the word *home* and another phone number. He was good-looking, employed, educated and probably not married or he wouldn't have given out his home phone. Four points in the positive column.

I stood there in my bedroom turning the card over and over and trying to decide what to do. If I gave it to Paula and pointed out that he obviously wanted her to call him, she'd crumple the card and toss it in the trash. Maybe even burn it and flush it. No retrieval possible.

Being married to a psycho abuser like her ex, David Bennett, was enough to make any woman reluctant to have another relationship. But I'd been married to Rickhead for five years and I'd jumped right back into the water when I met Trent. It was time for Paula to at least dip her toes in the shallow end.

I picked up my cell phone and punched in the handwritten number on the card.

"Hi. You've reached Matthew Graham. I'm not available at the moment but if you'll leave your name and number, I'll call you back."

"Hi, Matthew Graham. This is Lindsay Powell from Death by Chocolate where you had lunch today. Congratulations! You were our, uh, ten thousandth customer, and you've won a free chocolate dessert of your choice. Hope to see you at Death by Chocolate soon to enjoy your prize!"

Nobody can resist my chocolate concoctions. He'd be there.

Yes, that was a very pushy, controlling thing for me to do. I'm a pushy, controlling person. Deal with it.

I showered, grabbed some leftover Triple Chocolate Mousse Cake and headed for Fred's house. Henry walked with me but left as soon as Fred answered the door and he knew I was safe. He takes his guard-cat duties seriously. If anything happened to me, he'd have to figure out how to use the can opener, a difficult task with no opposable thumbs.

"Come in and join us," Fred invited. "Sophie's here and we're having coffee."

"Trade you chocolate for a Coke." I handed him the plastic container and went inside.

Looking beautiful in a soft blue blouse, matching ankle pants and sandals that showed off her dark red toenails, Sophie perched on Fred's leather sofa. "Lindsay, how nice to see you again and under better circumstances than the last time." She smiled but looked a little tense. Had I interrupted something more than a chat over coffee?

Nah, they couldn't be drinking coffee and doing anything intimate. Their breath would smell too awful.

Still I felt a little uncomfortable as I sat down next to Sophie. "Definitely a better day. We got our air conditioning at the shop fixed. Are you getting all settled in your new home?"

Fred appeared with a cold Coke and three plates holding slices of my mousse cake. I might have made something out of the fact that he was using his good china, but he always used good china. I'm not sure he even has anything else.

31

Fred took a seat in his recliner and sampled my cake. "Excellent as always." He turned his gaze to Sophie. "Lindsay makes the best desserts in the world, but don't ever drink coffee at her house."

It was all true so I couldn't feel insulted. What I did feel was a little left out. Fred's *my* friend. I'll share him but only if I can keep the number one slot, and I sensed secrets between Fred and Sophie.

Sophie took a bite of mousse and turned to me. "He's right. This is delicious."

"Thank you."

We all ate and drank in tense silence. Well, Sophie and I seemed tense. Fred didn't, of course.

Fred set his plate and fork on the coffee table. "Sophie remembered who Carolyn was."

Fred was including me in the secret. I felt better immediately.

"She was my imaginary friend when I was young." Sophie bit her lip and held the edge of her plate tightly. That was odd. Thoughts of my imaginary childhood friends, Augie Doggie and Topatee, always made me smile. Perhaps Carolyn hadn't been a particularly nice friend.

"I had imaginary friends," I said. "We had a lot of fun but we got into a lot of trouble too. They always did what I wanted and sometimes that didn't turn out so well, like the time we played pirates and buried my mother's jewelry in the back yard. I'm not sure whether Mom was more upset about her jewelry getting dirty or Dad about the mess I made in his golf-green lawn. Did you and Carolyn get in trouble?"

Sophie smiled tightly. "Yes, we did. We played dress up with Mother's clothes and makeup. We sneaked out at night and played hide and seek in the dark. The usual things kids do."

"But you forgot her completely until now?"

Fred tightened his lips and glared at me, letting me know I was being rude and pushy. I ignored him.

"It's normal to suppress memories after a traumatic incident like the death of her parents," he said.

I had just been reprimanded. I made a note to reprimand Fred later for reprimanding me.

"My aunt didn't encourage imaginary stories. Over the years, I guess I just moved it to the back of my mind."

"Do you remember what your imaginary friends looked like, Lindsay?" Fred asked.

"Sort of. Vaguely." *Not really.* "Is this another test? Do you remember what your imaginary friends looked like?" I was always trying to find out personal things about Fred and he was always refusing to tell me.

Of course he ignored my question. "Sophie remembers Carolyn very clearly."

Sophie nodded. "She had blond curly hair which I envied, blue eyes and fair skin. And her mother looked a lot like her."

"Your imaginary friend had a mother? My friends taunted me with the fact that they didn't have a mother and father who told them what to wear and when to go to bed and to finish their broccoli. Did your imaginary friends have parents, Fred?"

33

"When was the last time you saw your imaginary friends, Lindsay?" Fred asked, again ignoring my question.

I shrugged. "I don't know. I grew up and got interested in other things. It's not like they came by for a farewell party one day."

Fred looked at Sophie. She swallowed, leaned forward and carefully set her plate and fork on the coffee table. "I remember the last time I saw Carolyn. It was when she was murdered in Fred's bedroom."

Chapter Four

My fork rattled against my plate. I realized my fingers were twitching. I took a big gulp of Coke in an effort to swallow the shock rising in my throat. "You were in Fred's bedroom? You saw Carolyn get killed?"

I'm not an expert on imaginary friends, but I was pretty sure they didn't often die violent deaths. Only real friends did that.

"Maybe Carolyn wasn't imaginary," I said quietly. "Maybe she was a real person who lived in this house and you witnessed her murder."

Sophie gave a tight smile and shrugged. She was trying to appear nonchalant but it wasn't working. "I used to believe it really happened. I remember talking about it to my mother and father and then my aunt after my parents died. They all told me it was a dream, that Carolyn was imaginary. This house was vacant the whole time we lived here."

I looked at Fred questioningly, trying to ask him silently if that was true, if the house had been vacant.

He frowned. "Are you having a seizure, Lindsay?"

So much for my theory that he was psychic.

I turned back to Sophie. "You must have been in this house before. You knew your way around. You went straight to Fred's bedroom when you came here last night."

She nodded. "My mother said I loved to sneak over here and play, that I told her Carolyn and her mother lived here."

"I guess that makes sense. Mysterious, deserted house. Some kids would have populated it with witches and vampires and zombies."

Sophie's smile relaxed. "I was an only child, so I populated it with a best friend whose mother was a really good cook."

I looked at Fred again. He looked back with no expression. It was not possible he didn't see the absurdity of this conversation. Sophie's friend had to be real.

"Your imaginary friend had an imaginary mother who was a good cook? You ate over here, in an empty house? What did you eat?" *Dust?*

"I pretended we ate pizzas and hot dogs and ice cream. Carolyn's mother let us have all sorts of food we only got at my house for special occasions. Surely you had tea parties with your imaginary friends." She was beginning to sound a little defensive. I couldn't blame her. I was being nosy and tactless.

"Yes, we did have tea parties," I admitted. "But when Mother showed me how to pour air out of an empty teapot and pretend to drink from an empty teacup, I told her that was silly and demanded we have Coke and cookies for our tea parties."

"Your imaginary friends drank Coke and ate cookies?" Fred asked.

If that wasn't just like a man. Not a peep out of him when Sophie with her perfect skin and hair and eyes told an absurd tale about imaginary people and

36

imaginary food. Then he called me out on my imaginary friends? I'd let him know later what I thought of such behavior.

I lifted my chin and glared indignantly at him. "I ate and drank for them when Mother wasn't looking."

"And you think she didn't know that?"

"I think as long as I was sitting quietly, not making a mess, eating and conversing with people who didn't make a mess, she was happy. Sophie, did you have Carolyn over to your house for dinner?"

"Yes, I did."

"Did your mother set a plate for her?"

"Yes."

I leaned toward her, watching her expression carefully. "Did you eat her food for her?"

Sophie licked her lips and looked uncomfortable. "I guess so. It was a long time ago. Does it matter?"

Of course it mattered, but she didn't seem to want to deal with it. "Probably not."

She rose abruptly and smoothed her hands over her slacks. "I should go. Thank you for the coffee, Fred, and the cake, Lindsay. And again, I apologize for last night."

Fred and I both stood. I suddenly felt guilty about interrupting the two of them. Yeah, a minute ago I'd been jealous and desperate to insinuate myself into the conversation. But who knew the conversation was going to be so intense? So personal? "You don't need to leave," I protested. "I just came over to bring Fred his chocolate fix. I need to get home and, uh, feed my cat."

As if Henry heard me lying, a horrible noise came from Fred's front porch, a noise like a feral cat in the jungle about to take down a village. I'd heard that noise before, and it never meant anything good.

I dashed across the room and yanked open the front door just as Henry charged the screen and ripped it to shreds. I could only hope it hadn't been a treasured antique. Yeah, screen doors are usually rusty relics, but Fred's wasn't rusty though it didn't look new either. It was hard to tell with him.

Henry calmed as soon as he saw me. Well, at least he stopped yowling and being destructive. Instead he growled deep in his throat, paced to the edge of the porch then back to me, switching his tail the entire time. I opened what was left of the screen door and walked onto the porch. Henry trotted toward my house.

I looked in that direction and saw Rick hurrying down the sidewalk toward the black BMW convertible parked and running in the street.

"You have got to be kidding!" I protested to the universe.

I ran toward the car, but he got there before me. I barely had time to slap the trunk as he slid into the front seat and screeched away.

Henry trotted up, gave Rick's car a scathing look as it disappeared around the corner, then turned back toward the house, looking over his shoulder to be certain I was following. I stood for a moment grinding my teeth, wondering what Rick had done to my house that made him want to get away so fast. Only one way to find out. I followed my cat.

"We might need to call Trent and have him send out the bomb squad before we go near the house,

Henry. The way Rick peeled out of here, he may have left us a little present. Guess he wasn't happy that I refused to take care of his kid."

Henry trotted toward the porch and sat at the bottom of the steps, looking over his shoulder and grumbling deep in his throat. There was definitely something on that porch he didn't like.

"What's going on?"

Fred and Sophie were making their way through the uber-healthy vegetation in my yard, aka weeds. Fred held Sophie's arm protectively as if concerned she might stumble. Walking across my nonconforming yard, it was possible she might.

"Rick." I pointed down the street. "He made his getaway."

"What did he want?"

"May have planted a bomb."

Fred released Sophie's arm. "Stay here." He moved toward my house in long strides.

"I was kidding." I had to run to get to the porch before him. Why did I have to get there before him? I like being first.

Both of us stopped when we hit the second step up to the porch and were able to see what Rick had left for me.

Rickie sat on my porch swing, a long piece of red licorice in one hand, a Coke in the other. A battered, bulging canvas suitcase rested beside him.

No wonder Henry hadn't wanted to go on the porch.

"What are you doing here?" I already knew the answer to that question.

"My daddy said I was going to stay with you for two weeks and that you'd let me have all the Cokes and cookies I want. I want a cookie now."

Sophie caught up with us and stood beside Fred. "Who is this adorable child?"

"My ex-husband's son." I felt a little sorry for the kid, dropped off on one doorstep by his mother and on another by his father, but we had no time to waste. Rick could be planning to leave for the airport as soon as he got home and picked up Ginger. I pulled my keys from my pocket, grabbed Rickie's suitcase and headed toward the garage. "Come on. We're going back to your dad's."

"He's going out of town to make money to pay child support for me."

From the corner of my eye I saw Fred lift the boy bodily out of the swing and throw him over his shoulder.

I set the suitcase on the driveway and lifted my garage door then backed my Celica out. Fred opened the passenger door, slid the seat forward, put Rickie in the back seat, lifted the hatch, and tossed in his suitcase.

He held the passenger door open as he turned toward Sophie. "I apologize, but we have to leave for a few minutes. We'll be back shortly. The way Lindsay drives, this won't take long."

We'll be back shortly?

"Okay, I'll, uh, talk to you later." She sounded a little confused. Woman who sees imaginary playmate murdered meets woman who plans to murder ex-husband. We all have our little idiosyncrasies.

40

"Close the door!" I shouted.

He slid into the passenger seat and complied with my order. "Go," he said. "If you want to get this boy to Rick's house before he leaves, you need to press on the accelerator and make this car move. Nobody's going to beam you over there."

"You can't ride with me! You hate riding with me!"

"My life insurance is paid up."

Even with the time constraints, I couldn't resist the chance to find out something about Fred. "Who's the beneficiary?"

"Do you really want to sit here and talk while Rick's getting away?"

I hit the gas, backed out to the street, threw the car into gear and peeled out.

"I spilled my Coke," Rickie whined from the back seat.

Great. I knew from experience how difficult it was to get Coke out of the upholstery.

Rick would probably volunteer to clean it for me since his son did it. Yeah, I get sarcastic even in my thoughts.

"I don't want to go to my dad's," Rickie complained. "I don't like that woman who lives there."

"Big deal. Neither do I."

"Have you met Rick's new girlfriend?" Fred asked.

"No, but if Rick likes her, I'm pretty sure I don't." I slid around a corner on two and a half wheels.

Sally Berneathy

Rick drives a hot car, but it's all for show. I easily caught up to him and pulled in behind him as he sat in his driveway waiting for his garage door to go up.

Of course he saw me. He pulled into the garage and immediately started the door on its downward journey. But those doors are slow. I slid out of my car and ran under before it got halfway down. Apparently I tripped the electric beam because the door stopped then went back up.

Rick jumped from his car. "Get out of my house!"

"Just as soon as I return what belongs to you."

Fred ambled up beside me, Rickie in tow. Rick paled when he saw Fred. "What are you doing here?"

"Returning your son." Fred's voice betrayed no hint of the insanity in progress. He might have been referring to a piece of mail delivered to the wrong address.

The door to the house opened and a triple D blonde stepped out. "Honey, what's going on? Who are those people?"

"Go back inside, Ginger. I'll be there in a minute."

Her bottom lip...another triple D implant...pouted. "I thought you were taking the kid to a babysitter so we could be alone."

"I'll take care of it. Go back inside."

I recognized his tone. He had given an order and if she didn't comply, she'd be in trouble. I was much more familiar with what happened when I didn't

42

comply with Rick's demands than with what happened when I did since I rarely did.

I strode toward Ginger, extending my hand. She moved backward, looking at Rick as if for directions on how to handle this latest atrocity. "Hi, I'm Lindsay, the ex. So nice to meet Rickie's latest stepmother. Did you know Rick's buying another ticket to Hawaii so you can go together as one big happy family?"

Her eyes widened. "You said it would be just us, Rick!"

"She's lying," Rick assured her.

I smiled. "Just kidding."

"Go inside, Ginger. I'll take care of this."

She opened her mouth as if she was going to protest, but instead blinked and obediently went back into the house, closing the door behind her.

Rick turned on his salesman's hundred watt smile. "Lindsay, please, this one time, do this favor for me. We have to leave for the airport at four in the morning. How am I going to find a babysitter by then?"

I looked at Fred. "Do you know the answer to that question?"

"No."

I turned back to Rick. "Okay. I've asked the audience and I don't want to phone a friend. I guess I'll have to give up on that question. I have no idea. Good luck!"

Fred took my arm and we started out of the garage.

I turned back. "If you ever pull this kind of a stunt again, I'll call social services. Do you want your son in a foster home?"

The look on Rick's face told me that was a wasted threat. He didn't care if his son went into a foster home just as long as he didn't have to be bothered with him. Now that I'd given him the idea, he might call social services just to get a babysitter. Damn.

"Daddy, she didn't give me any cookies. You said she'd give me cookies."

I could feel Rick seething behind me. Maybe he'd get so angry he'd explode. I walked a little faster so none of the pieces would hit me.

As I backed down Rick's driveway, my brain registered the car on the far side of the garage. Ginger's, I assumed. It was one of those really small cars and the color was blue, not white. Definitely not the car I'd seen last night parked under the trees with a blond haired man at the wheel.

I smiled as I thought of what that could mean. Was Rick already cheating on Ginger with a woman who drove a white sedan?

Or maybe it hadn't been Rick, just a stranger parked on my street at two o'clock in the morning. That sounded a little creepy.

Of the two possibilities, I found myself hoping it was Rick being his usual obnoxious but relatively harmless self. I suppose that's sort of like saying I'd prefer to be run over by a bus instead of a train.

Chapter Five

Henry and I both had a restless night. He usually sleeps quite soundly, so when he got up to look out the bedroom window in the middle of the night, I got up too.

Sophie, wearing the same or a similar white nightgown, moved like a ghost through the moonlight across the street to Fred's house. He must have been expecting her because he opened the door as soon as she reached it.

Sleepwalking or a tryst?

I'd never known Fred to have a girlfriend. Of course, he's so secretive, he could have had a different one every night for all I knew.

But a couple of minutes later Fred and Sophie came out of the house together. He walked her back to her house, one arm wrapped protectively around her waist. She turned at her door, looked up at him and smiled then gave him a quick kiss on the cheek.

Fred blushed. Okay, it was dark and they were on her porch under the overhang, so I couldn't really see the color of his face but I'm pretty sure it got red.

"We can go back to bed, Henry. Fred's got the situation under control. He doesn't need us."

And that was a good thing. I was glad Fred didn't call me to come over in the middle of the night and help him get Sophie out of his closet again. But I have to admit, I felt a little left out.

Fred paused in the middle of the street, looked up toward my bedroom window and waved.

I waved back even though I was certain he couldn't see me in the darkness. But if he couldn't see me, why did he wave in the first place? More of the mystery that was Fred.

Henry and I went back to bed, but he got me up again half an hour later.

My quiet neighborhood was busy that night.

It was the white sedan again, driving slowly down the street. From my angle at the upstairs bedroom window, I couldn't see who was in the car. Male, female, blond, brunette, monster, alien?

The car slowed almost to a stop in front of my house. Henry and I both leaned forward, watching intently. I half expected the passenger door to open and Rick to shove Rickie out of it. But after a significant hesitation, it moved on.

Department of Health checking on my lawn? Rick had sent them after me once. But they probably didn't sneak around in the middle of the night. The city would have to pay the employees overtime. That wasn't going to happen.

Henry's first family looking for him in the middle of the night? When he'd showed up and moved in, I'd put signs everywhere and nobody claimed him. After all this time, he was my cat and I was his can opener. Nobody was going to separate us, not even with a DNA test.

The cat in question turned away from the window and sauntered over to the bed. He wasn't worried.

I went back to bed too and had almost dozed off again when a strange thought occurred to me.

Perhaps the white sedan wasn't stopping in front of my house. Perhaps it was stopping in front of Sophie's house. We were right across the street from each other. And that woman had secrets, lots of secrets, secrets she was keeping from herself even.

Maybe she'd killed Carolyn. That could be traumatic enough to give her nightmares and cause her to walk in her sleep.

A five year old dark haired kindergartener wearing a clown mask and wielding a bloody butcher knife?

Probably not.

I pulled the sheet over my head and ordered my mind to stop playing games and let me go back to sleep.

When I left for work that morning I halfway expected to find Rickie sitting in my porch swing. Nothing there but a small bit of Rickie's candy and a few ants.

The happy couple should be on their way to the airport. Maybe they'd decided to take the kid along after all.

I laughed at my own joke.

❧

Paula and I prepared to feed the hungry masses. I made half a dozen Double Chocolate Cream Pies. The masses needed chocolate.

While Paula flailed away at the cinnamon roll dough and I beat cream for the topping, I told her about Sophie and Fred's middle of the night encounter.

Paula spread the dough on a marble board and picked up her institutional size rolling pin. "I've never thought about Fred being involved in a relationship."

I added sugar to the whipping cream. "He may have three wives and six children living across town. It's hard to know about Fred."

"I can see why he'd be attracted to Sophie. She's beautiful."

"And mysterious. Fred's a sucker for a mystery."

Paula laughed. "Fred's a sucker for a beautiful face, a soft voice and big—"

"Don't say it!" I pictured Ginger's triple Ds. I didn't want to think of any comparison between her and Sophie. Totally different people.

"Big brown eyes," Paula finished. "What'd you think I was going to say?"

"Nothing. Pass me the vanilla."

"Fred deserves somebody special in his life."

"He has you, me and Zach. It doesn't get any more special than us."

Paula handed me the bottle of vanilla. "You know what I mean. You have Fred, Zach and me, but Trent fills a different place in your life."

I couldn't deny that. I'd thought I'd never become involved in another male/female relationship after being married to Rickhead and having my emotions beaten up, bullied and abused. But my feelings for Trent had sort of snuck up on me. Okay, maybe I shied away from examining those feelings too closely or putting a label on them, but whatever

Trent and I had going on was good. It made me happy. I wanted Paula to find that same happiness.

"You're right," I said. "Fred does deserve to have someone special in his life. And so do you."

She turned back to her dough and gave it a vicious whack with that rolling pin. I flinched. "When I get Zach raised, I'll think about it."

She had no intention of thinking about it. I could only imagine how terrified she must be of ever trusting another man after the abusive, psychotic, murderous jerk she'd been married to. What I'd gone through with Rick was awful but nothing compared to the nightmare she'd lived through.

My efforts to get Matthew Graham back to talk to her again could be wasted. He could fail to show. She might not talk to him again. He could show up and be a creep. Anything or nothing could happen.

But what if I'd refrained from getting involved with Trent because he was a cop and cops cause me a lot of grief by giving me all those unjustified speeding tickets? What if I'd taken Henry to a homeless shelter instead of adopting him?

Sometimes you have to take chances.

I let the subject drop, and we had a good day. Lots of people for breakfast, lots of people for lunch. Nobody died, nobody dropped off their kid and ran away. A very good day.

The lunch crowd was winding down when Matthew Graham, Associate Professor of History, came in and sat down at the counter.

Yes!

Paula was serving at the far end of the counter and I was heading back to the kitchen with a tray of dirty dishes. Before I could dispose of the dishes, Paula moved down to take his order.

I really needed to get there first and do the free dessert thing.

He smiled at her. He had a nice smile, open and guileless. "I got your call about being your ten thousandth customer." Pleasant voice. Soft.

She frowned. "What?"

Still clutching my tray of dirty dishes, I moved over beside her and gave Matthew my biggest smile. "Welcome! I'm so glad you came in! What would you like for your free dessert today? We have chocolate chip cookies, brownies and our special today, Double Chocolate Cream Pie with real whipped cream. The cookies and brownies have nuts. Sometimes we have cookies and brownies without nuts but today is a total nuts day. The pie has no nuts, though sometimes we have a wonderful fudge pie with nuts, but not today."

Paula gripped my arm. Tightly. I stopped babbling.

"Why don't you just take your time, sir," she said, "and look over the desserts in the case to your right. If you'd like to order something besides dessert, we have grilled chicken sandwiches and hamburgers." With the hand that wasn't cutting off the blood in my arm, she indicated the chalk board behind us. "We'll be back to take your order in a few minutes. Lindsay, let me help you carry that heavy tray to the kitchen."

Busted.

We marched back to the kitchen and I set the dishes in the sink.

"You called that man and told him he was our ten thousandth customer and he should come in for a free dessert?" Paula accused in an angry whisper.

When I'd conceived the brilliant plan to get Matthew Graham back to the restaurant to talk to Paula, I hadn't really thought it through. Sometimes I act a little impulsively. The plan did work. I just hadn't considered the possibility that Paula would get to him before I could set things up.

I drew a deep breath and tried to think of something that would explain what I'd done, something other than the truth, of course.

"Yes, I did call him. He is our ten thousandth customer."

"That's ridiculous! We don't have any system to count customers."

"I have a really good memory."

"Not that good. How did you get his name and phone number?"

I squirmed and looked around for a Coke. Even an old flat one would help. "He left his business card."

She threw her hands into the air. "So you called him and told him an outrageous lie to get him back in here? Why?"

"Why?" When stalling for time, answer a question with a question, even if it's the same question.

"I'm going to take a wild guess. You didn't do it because you're finally free of Rick and want to

51

explore the possibilities out there in the single world. You seem very happy with Trent."

"Explore the possibilities? No! I am totally happy with Trent."

"So my next wild guess is that you saw me talking to Matthew yesterday and decided to bring him back for me to play with."

When all else fails, tell the truth. "I wouldn't put it exactly like that. You seemed to be having a good time and he left his card which meant he wanted to see you again and I knew you'd never call him."

She nodded. "You are correct. I would not have called him because I don't want to talk to him."

"He seems really nice."

"Yes, he does, which makes it very bad that you lied to him."

I shrugged. "He's getting a free dessert out of it. That should make up for a teeny, tiny little lie."

She turned to the sink and began rinsing the dishes. "Then go serve him his free dessert and get rid of him."

I thought about that but only for a moment. "No." I picked up the rinsed plates and put them in the dishwasher.

"What?"

"I'm not going out there to take his order. You can be rude and let him sit there until we're ready to close then run him off, or you can go see what the nice man wants to eat."

She was silent for a moment. With a sigh she dried her hands and started toward the entrance to the front area, turning back at the door. "I won't forget this."

I smiled. "You mean like I didn't forget those first nine thousand nine hundred ninety nine customers?"

We have a swinging door between the restaurant area and the kitchen so she couldn't slam it behind her, but she tried.

She'd thank me later.

Or maybe not, but she'd never know if she didn't give it a shot.

∂∾∾

The two of them talked while he ate his chicken sandwich and chocolate cookie. I even caught her smiling once or twice. He dallied over that cookie a long time, waiting for everyone else to leave so he could talk to Paula some more.

Finally he left. Paula locked the front door and put up the "Closed" sign.

I'd already done most of the cleanup in the front area since that gave me the opportunity to eavesdrop. When I went back to the kitchen, I expected Paula to join me to clean in there. She didn't. I looked out to see her wiping down tables I'd already wiped down, filling napkin holders I'd already filled.

She finally came back to get the bucket and mop.

"You seemed to enjoy talking to him," I said.

She glared at me and went back to the front. I chose to interpret that as meaning she had enjoyed the experience but didn't want to admit it. Sometimes she refuses to confide in me. Took her over a year to admit she'd killed her husband. She hadn't, of course, which was a shame. But that just goes to show she's as secretive as Fred. My two best friends, and they both keep secrets while I tell everybody everything.

I'd done my part. Now I could only wait to see if Matthew came back and if she talked to him again.

I returned home that afternoon to find my porch swing still unoccupied. Even the bit of candy and the ants were gone.

I fed Henry and let him outside then took a Double Chocolate Cream Pie over to Fred's. I often took chocolate to Fred, but this was sort of a bribe. Although Matthew seemed nice enough and I liked his looks and smile, I probably ought to have him checked out before I meddled any more.

Fred opened the door as soon as I stepped onto the porch. He'd seen me coming with his x-ray vision.

I handed him Matthew Graham's card. "Can you check this guy out? See if he has any wants, warrants or wives?"

He accepted the card and held the screen door open. It looked identical to the one he'd always had, but it no longer showed signs of Henry's claws. "Did you magically heal this door?"

"Of course not. I had it replaced. Sometimes you say the strangest things."

"Yeah, well, sometimes you do the strangest things."

I went over to sit on his sofa. A cold can of Coke waited for me on a coaster on the coffee table and a steaming cup of coffee sat on the lamp table beside his recliner.

He took the pie to the kitchen and returned with slices for both of us. After handing a plate to me, he sat in his recliner and took a bite, chewed thoughtfully and swallowed. "Very good. Thank you. Why do you want me to check out this person?"

"He's been in the shop a couple of times and he seems to be interested in Paula." He didn't really need to know the long version.

Fred studied the card then tucked it into his shirt pocket. "Good idea. After what she went through with her psychotic ex, we need to do everything we can to protect her."

"Now tell me what happened last night."

"You saw what happened. Sophie came to my door, I woke her and walked her home."

"I saw the outside part. I didn't see what happened in your house. Did she do the crying and screaming thing again?"

He frowned, sipped his coffee and nodded. "Yes, she was quite upset. I'm not so sure moving back here was a wise decision on her part."

"That's strange. She said she moved back because she had happy memories of living here, but as soon as she gets here, she starts having bad dreams."

"Very strange." Fred had another bite of pie and another sip of coffee.

I waited, but when he forked another piece, I interrupted. "Well? So what do you make of that?"

He finished his bite before replying. Of course he couldn't leave it halfway through the process. "There's no way to be certain at this point, but I think on a subconscious level, she was driven to return here to find out what happened to Carolyn."

"So we're going on the assumption that Carolyn was a real person and Sophie witnessed her murder, right?"

Fred set his empty plate on the lamp table and leaned back in his chair. "More than likely Sophie witnessed a real murder, and her nightmares won't stop until we uncover the truth. Our first step is to figure out who was murdered."

"What do you mean, who? A little girl named Carolyn. Surely with your hacking skills you can find out if someone named Carolyn lived in this house and died a violent death twenty years ago."

He nodded. "I searched the records for the occupants of this house during the time Sophie and her parents lived across the street."

"And?"

"Sophie's right. The house was vacant."

I scowled. "So maybe Carolyn lived in another house in the neighborhood and she and Sophie played in this house the way she said except Carolyn wasn't imaginary. Maybe some psycho killer came in one day and murdered Carolyn while Sophie watched."

"I searched all records for five years prior to the time Sophie and her parents left town and found no record of the death of a young child in Pleasant Grove during that time."

"Are you saying Carolyn really *was* imaginary? That Sophie made up the whole thing?"

"We have to consider that possibility."

Somehow that just didn't feel right. I'd seen the terror on Sophie's face. Of course, I've had a few nightmares myself. The terror at the time always seems very real. "Well," I said, "if there's no mystery to solve, then we can't find any answers for Sophie so I guess she'll continue to come over to your house in the middle of the night."

"That's a possibility." He stood and picked up his plate. "I think I'll have another piece of pie. Would you like one?"

"What? Oh, no, thanks." I was trying to wrap my head around the possibility that Sophie's distress was all imaginary. She seemed so down to earth, so well-adjusted—except for running around in her sleep and ending up in a strange man's closet.

"Would you like to come with me tomorrow to question the man who owned this house during that time?"

"No, thanks." Then I realized we were no longer on the subject of pie. "What?" He was disappearing into the kitchen. I ran after him.

"What did you just say?"

He meticulously sliced a piece of pie. "I asked if you'd like to participate in questioning the previous owner of this house, the one who owned it for five years and kept it unoccupied the entire time." He moved the piece of pie to his plate.

"I thought..." What had I thought? He'd said the house was vacant, but of course somebody had owned it. "Yes, I want to go. When? Who am I going to be? What shall I wear?"

"Tomorrow as soon as you get off work. Look professional. You're going to be a mold expert."

I was pretty sure he said *mold expert*, not *moldy expert*. But one never knows with Fred.

Chapter Six

I left Fred's house and headed toward Paula's to share the latest news.

Near the end of the block I saw Zach pedaling his red and yellow tricycle hard and fast down the sidewalk. My first thought was that Paula had come a long way over the last couple of years, letting Zach play outside by himself. But then I saw her standing on her front porch watching him. She still guarded her son and her heart closely. I was fighting an uphill battle with the Matthew thing.

As I crossed my yard, Henry appeared from nowhere and joined me. "You want to go see Zach, don't you?" I asked him. He often pretended indifference toward the boy, but he pretends indifference toward everybody. I knew Henry and Zach were friends. They chased lightning bugs together and Zach dropped bits of everything he ate so Henry could eat them or ignore them as suited his fancy.

"I have to tell Paula about Fred discovering that the house really was vacant." He looked up at me, disbelief in his big blue eyes. "Okay, yes, I want to ask her about Matthew too. There's no point in my pursuing this thing with him if she doesn't even like him."

Henry moved on through the grass, curling his tail in a gesture of smug pleasure that he'd forced me to admit the truth. Like I'd ever lie to my cat.

Zach reached the end of the block, made a U-turn and headed back. He saw me and waved. "Anlinny!"

"You're going to get a ticket for going that fast, Hot Shot!" I called.

Paula turned her attention to me as I approached her house. She looked much more relaxed and happy than she had at the restaurant. Being with her son always made her happy.

"Hi!" I greeted.

Zach rode toward me, slowing when he hit the grass but still pedaling as hard as he could. When he reached me, he jumped off the bike and grabbed me around the legs, looking up at me with a huge grin. "We're gonna have macaroni and cheese! You can eat with us!"

"Henry too?"

He giggled. "Henry eats cat food."

"Among other things." I thought it best not to mention the occasional mouse my cat consumed and sometimes offered to share with me.

We went inside where Zach's toys added splashes of bright color to the uniform beige of Paula's living room. Two years after her ex-husband's capture and conviction, she'd finally opened the blinds to allow the sunlight inside. That was a start.

"Read while I finish making dinner." She handed him a large, colorful children's book.

He sank to the floor, opened the book and began reciting a tale about zombies and mutant bunny rabbits. Nothing to do with ham and green eggs or Bambi or wild things. Nothing remotely related to the book he held in his hands. The boy has a vivid imagination. Henry sat beside him, switching his tail and pretending to be engrossed in the story. Maybe he wasn't pretending.

I followed Paula into the kitchen. She filled a pot with water and set it on the stove to boil. I helped myself to a Coke from her refrigerator and sat down at her kitchen table.

"Nobody lived in Fred's house when Sophie was five years old," I said. "But Fred's found the owner and we're going to talk to him tomorrow."

"The house really was vacant?" She took lettuce and tomatoes from the refrigerator and set them on a chopping board. "So Sophie's telling the truth? Her friend Carolyn was imaginary?"

I shook my head. "I don't think so. But we're going to find out. Fred believes she can't get over her trauma until she learns the truth about what happened in that house."

She took down three salad bowls. Apparently I was invited to dinner and I'd have to eat my greens. It would be worth it. Paula's a good cook. "So she's going to keep coming over to Fred's house in the middle of the night until you figure it out or she remembers?"

"I guess so. Of course, we have no proof that Fred objects to a beautiful woman visiting every night. Can I help you do something?"

She took a large knife from a wooden block on the counter. "Thanks, but I'm not making anything chocolate and you have a way of, um, changing the outcome when you cook anything not chocolate."

I couldn't deny that. My desserts are all wonderful, but my biscuits are like rocks and my coffee is like swamp water. Not that I've ever tasted swamp water. I do make a great can of Coke, however.

"I'm having Fred check out Matthew Graham."

Paula slammed the knife into the tomato so hard I was afraid she'd chop through the board and the counter. "Why would you do that?"

"It's probably not necessary. Just a precaution. He seems nice and has a really sweet smile and being a college professor, that's a good thing—"

"Stop!" Another solid chop to the board, cutting through a piece of lettuce. She compressed her lips and shook her head. "Lindsay, if you weren't my best friend, you would be my worst enemy. I have no desire to meet someone. I don't need to meet someone. Zach doesn't need strange men coming and going and confusing him."

"No problem. I totally understand why you've been a little reluctant to get involved with somebody after what David did to you. That's why Fred's checking out Matthew, to avoid the strange men."

She shuddered, carefully laid the knife on the board and looked at me. "I don't think you do understand."

I spread my hands in a *duh* gesture. "I've seen your scars. I know how terrified you were when you moved here. I was there when he tried to take Zach. I was there when he tried to kill me."

She leaned back against the counter and drew in a deep breath. "I realize you know all that. You know he abused me, hurt me and tried to hurt Zach. You know he let me think I'd killed him and then tried to get me sent to prison so he could take Zach from me."

"He's a monster," I agreed. "But he's in prison. He's gone. You have to move on with your life."

She arched an eyebrow. "I'm moving on just fine. I have a wonderful son, a great job, a best friend and a neighbor who sneaks around in the dark and does weird things."

I scowled. "If you're talking about Fred, he does weird things in the daytime too."

She laughed. "I was talking about Henry, but Fred's a part of my life too. I'm happy. What more could any woman want?"

"How about somebody special? Somebody to be a father to Zach. Somebody to hold you at night and..." I waved my hands vaguely through the air. "You know. Maybe someday have a brother or sister for Zach."

She shook her head. "You don't understand. I thought I loved David." Her voice was suddenly so quiet I had to strain to hear her words. "I had nobody. My parents were dead. I was alone. David came along, and I thought I loved him. It took him a while to kill that love, to hurt me so badly that I stopped loving him. Every time he hit me, every time he said something mean, he destroyed a piece of my heart. Finally, there was nothing left to destroy. Lindsay, even if I wanted to, I simply don't have the ability to love somebody again."

I was silent for a long moment, kept my mouth shut and refrained from saying, *What a crock.* Oh, she believed it. I had no doubt of her sincerity. But I knew different. She was still a kind, loving person in spite of what David Bennett had done to her.

I took her proclamation as a challenge. If Matthew didn't work out, I'd find somebody else to audition for the part of Paula's Special Person. There were about two million people in the Kansas City metropolitan area. Surely somewhere I could find the right guy for Paula. If not, St. Louis isn't that far away when you drive like I do.

Zach charged into the kitchen. "Mama, Henry's hungry!"

She picked up her son and kissed the top of his sweaty head. "It won't be long. Water's boiling. Just give me a few more minutes."

"Okay." He wriggled, trying to get down.

She set him on the floor. "I love you."

"I love you too. Can I have a Coke, Anlinny?"

"Of course." I went to the cabinet, took down a red plastic glass and filled it with cranberry juice.

Zach took the glass but looked suspiciously at what I was drinking. "I want mine in a can like yours."

Boy was growing up.

He needed a father.

I accepted the challenge.

ॐঔ

Matthew came to Death by Chocolate the next day. Two o'clock, end of the lunch rush, an hour from closing time. As soon as he came in the front door, I went into the kitchen where Paula was loading the dishwasher.

"Can you take the front for a few minutes? I need to make a phone call."

She closed the dishwasher door and looked at me through narrowed eyes. "He's out there, isn't he?"

"Who?"

"You know very well who I'm talking about."

I pulled my cell phone from my pocket. "Got to call Fred. We're going to visit the previous owner of his house." That was all true. I just didn't mention that I needed to call Fred to get the report on Matthew Graham.

I went through the back door to the alley, giving her no choice but to go out front.

I called Fred. "Did you check on Matthew Graham?"

"Yes."

"And?"

"Squeaky clean. Doesn't even have any speeding tickets."

"You say that like it's something commendable."

He sighed. "Some people might think so. Anyway, this guy checks out down the line. Single, never been married. Got his PhD in history from the University of Missouri in Columbia. Graduated with honors. He grew up around this area and his family still lives here."

"Tell me about his family."

"Mother and father still alive, still married. Matthew is the youngest of eight kids. Seven boys and one girl."

"Wow. That's a lot of family."

"They're members of Seventh Gate. They have large families."

I cringed. "That name sounds familiar. Isn't that some kind of a nut job religious group?"

"Yes, it is. Those people give new meaning to the word *strange*. It was started back in the sixties by a guy named Gary Drummond who got carried away with the hallucinogenic drugs. He was certain the Apocalypse was just around the corner so he bought some land which was dirt cheap in those days and set up his own patriarchal cult on a self-sustaining farm. They're still out there, waiting for the end. It appears Matthew escaped when he was eighteen."

"So I take it he's not close to his family?" I hoped not.

"Once somebody leaves there, that person is dead to them, so I assume they're not close. It's difficult to find out a lot about them. They refuse to file any sort of documents with the government, no birth certificates, no tax returns, no social security numbers. They consider the government, technology, and all of us to be satanic. The FBI, ATF and IRS have tried to take them down, but so far they haven't made a lot of progress. They get away with a lot under the umbrella of religious freedom."

"But Matthew ran away. That speaks well for his sanity. His past doesn't matter. Is he dating anybody?

Did you hack into his cell phone to see if he's been sending nude pictures of himself to somebody?"

"His Facebook status does not indicate he's in a relationship and I didn't find any e-mails or texts that indicate he's romantically involved with anyone. As far as I can determine, he's not sending nude pictures of himself to anybody through any form of modern technology. As to whether he's taking them with an old-fashioned camera and handing them to someone in person, I have no idea."

"Okay, thanks. Gotta run. See you in a couple of hours to begin our other investigation."

I disconnected the call and dashed through the kitchen into the restaurant. Matthew and Paula were the only people there. She was leaning over the counter toward him. He was leaning toward her. They both jerked upright and looked at me when I entered the room.

"Paula and I are having a cookout at my place tomorrow evening, Matthew. Would you like to come?"

Paula gasped.

Matthew blinked rapidly, looked from me to Paula, bit his lip then finally nodded. "Yes, thank you. I'd love to come. Can I bring something? I have a friend who grows fresh watermelons."

"Sounds great." I scrawled my address on the back of an order form and handed it to him. "Six o'clock on Saturday. See you then."

"I look forward to it." He gave me a big smile then turned his attention to Paula and gave her a really big smile, his blue gray eyes warm. It was pretty obvious he had a thing for her.

She returned his smile. Not quite as warmly, but it was better than a frown.

She walked to the door with him and locked up.

I felt certain Paula was secretly pleased that I'd invited Matthew to join us for the cookout, but she managed to keep her pleasure secret. In fact, she pretended to be a little miffed. "I can't believe you did that, especially not after our talk last night."

"Hey, worst case scenario, you decide you don't like him but we get to eat fresh watermelon. The ones they have at the grocery store are disgusting."

We cleaned while I told her the details of Matthew's life that Fred had uncovered. She slammed the dishwasher door, pressed her lips together tightly then looked at me in an obvious attempt to appear unimpressed with my due diligence.

I had a good feeling about Matthew Graham, and my feelings are rarely wrong.

Well, okay, there was the whole Rick thing. But I've honed my people skills since then.

<u>Chapter Seven</u>

I rushed home to prepare for a busy evening.

First I had to be a moldy expert with Fred, and then Trent would be over since it was Friday. Of course, my first priority was Henry's nutritional needs. With that taken care of, I showered and changed into a white blouse, black slacks and matching jacket then went over to Fred's.

He waited in his driveway beside his classic white Mercedes, holding the passenger door open. I always felt I should dust off my clothes and wipe my feet before I got in that car.

I slid in and fastened my seat belt though I saw no reason to do so. In fact, I never understood why he'd gone to the trouble to add seat belts to a classic car in the first place. He insists on driving the speed limit. With his hacking skills, he could probably erase any speeding tickets he got. Completely inexplicable.

"Is that the same black suit you always wear or do you have an endless supply of them?" He guided the car slowly around a corner.

"Just the one. I only wear it to funerals and to visit mob bosses, private eyes and hookers with you. Nobody's died lately and this is the first fact-finding mission we've gone on in several months, so it's not getting a lot of use. Tell me about the guy we're going to talk to. What do I need to know about him? Mob boss? Crooked cop? Drug dealer?"

Fred managed to give me a strange look even though he would never take his eyes off the road. "This man's name is Daniel Jamison, and he's a doctor."

Great. I was going to have to lie to somebody who spent his days healing people. What kind of bad Karma was that going to bring down on my head?

"What kind of doctor? Philosophy? Physics?" Lying to that kind of a doctor wouldn't be so bad.

"The medical kind. He's a surgeon."

Terrific. "Spends his days cutting out malignant growths and saving lives?"

"Not exactly. He spends his days making people beautiful. He's a cosmetic surgeon."

I wondered if he'd been the one who did my mother's little nips and tucks. If so, he deserved to be lied to. It's just wrong when a mother looks younger than her daughter.

≈⊷≋s

Doctor Daniel Jamison's office was on the Kansas side in an elite area. We entered the four story building and took the hushed elevator to the fourth floor which also felt hushed. Money buys a lot of silence.

"I'm amazed you were able to get us in to see any doctor on such short notice." We stepped from the elevator onto the burgundy carpet of the hallway. "They make me wait a month or two."

"I didn't just call and ask for an appointment."

70

Of course he didn't. How silly of me to think Fred would do anything that mundane.

I didn't ask any more questions, but the next time I had a sinus infection, I'd definitely be asking for his help.

We entered Dr. Jamison's plush waiting room and the receptionist immediately showed us into his plush office.

A man in a pristine white coat rose from behind a large desk when we entered. He was a tall, dark haired, good-looking guy of about forty. Maybe fifty, depending on how much work he'd traded with colleagues.

"Dr. Sommers." He shook Fred's hand.

Oboy. Now Fred was impersonating a doctor.

"Dr. Jamison," Fred acknowledged then turned to me. "And this is Lindsay Powell."

Jamison offered his hand to me. His fingers were big and gentle. I had expected long, thin fingers, but perhaps I was getting surgeons confused with piano players. "So you believe you've found stachybotrys chartarum in the house I used to own in Pleasant Grove?"

"Uh…" I said.

Stachybotrys chartarum?

Fred sat in one of the chairs in front of the doctor's desk and pulled me down to the other one. "In the basement," he said. "No real problem. Ms. Powell is sure she can get rid of it. But I'm preparing to sell the house and I want to be certain I give full disclosure about everything. You know how obsessive people are about that sort of thing these days."

71

Jamison nodded and sat in his large leather chair. "I do understand. There's so much liability attached to anything we do anymore." He folded his hands on his desk. The only other objects on the desk were pictures of a beautiful blond woman and two beautiful kids at various ages, babies to young adults. He was a family man. That was nice. "I can assure you there was no mold when I owned the house."

Fred nodded. "You're certain? This mold appears to have been around for a while."

"Old mold," I contributed.

Both men looked at me. Perhaps I should have refrained from giving my expert opinion, but I was the mold expert. I cleared my throat. "Determining the age of mold is my specialty. Molds can be very clever about hiding their age. Sometimes it's like they get a face lift."

Jamison smiled tentatively as if uncertain whether I was joking.

Fred turned his attention back to the doctor. "Was there any flooding in the basement when you lived there? The big flood of 1993 caused a lot of problems in basements around this area."

Jamison's tanned face seemed to pale but maybe it was just an illusion of the soft, indirect lighting in the room. However, he definitely clenched his hands a little tighter.

A flood phobia? Worried the mold was going to be another liability for him? I wondered if he had many of those, if he had pictures on one of those Plastic Surgery Gone Wrong websites.

"I never had a problem with that basement." Jamison unclenched his hands and pulled a picture closer. The picture featured a younger version of him with the blond woman and two small children. "It was always dry. No flooding."

"How long did you and your family live there?" It was a loaded question since we knew he hadn't lived there at all. He already seemed nervous. Maybe I could push another button.

A sheen of sweat appeared on his unlined forehead. "We never lived there. I bought the house as an investment." He kept his focus on the picture. My mother would have smacked his wrists for such bad manners.

"An investment? I see. It would be a really big help if we could talk to the people who rented from you," I said.

Fred gave me a barely perceptible nod of approval. I was getting good at the deceit business.

Jamison shook his head. "I didn't rent it to anyone." He still didn't look at me.

"Nobody in the five years you owned it?"

Again he shook his head. "Nobody."

"It sat empty all that time? That doesn't sound like a very good investment."

He finally lifted his gaze and gave a small, phony smile. "You're right. It wasn't a very good investment. Lee's Summit became the hot area, not Pleasant Grove."

"Even so, I'm surprised you couldn't find anybody to rent it in five years."

Fred frowned and I wondered if I was pushing Jamison too hard. I'd left the topic of mold far behind and was verging on nosiness.

Jamison licked his lips. "I was in med school at the time. My wife and I were having some problems. I planned to move into the house myself but…" He shrugged and tried the phony smile again. "We worked things out." He checked his watch and stood. "If you need me to sign some sort of document specifying there was no mold in the house when I owned it, I'll be happy to do so but right now I have another appointment."

Fred rose. "I don't think that will be necessary, but thank you for the offer. I'll let you know if it comes to that."

We started out of the office which had gone from hushed to almost vibrating with Jamison's tension.

Fred turned back at the door. "One of the neighbors, Sophie Fleming, three story Victorian house across the street and up one, has found some mold problems too. Did you know them? The Flemings?"

He swallowed and his throat convulsed as if he was choking. "No." The word came out as a loud whisper. "I never met them."

I looked at Fred. "Was that the family with the little girl? Carolyn? Wasn't that her name?"

"No," Fred replied, "Carolyn was somebody else."

Indirect lighting or not, Jamison's face went several shades paler.

Fred smiled. "Thank you for your time."

He also thanked the receptionist on our way out.

I enjoyed it when Fred did that. Slice them, dice them, make them sweat, but always with perfect manners.

I restrained myself until we were out of the cool, hushed building and back in the hot, noisy parking lot.

"He knows something!" I said as Fred emerged from the revolving door behind me.

He lifted an eyebrow. "He knows lots of things or he wouldn't be licensed to perform surgery."

I punched his arm. "Stop that! You know what I mean!"

He smiled and opened the car door for me.

To my amazement, Fred's perfect vehicle had the audacity to be hot and steamy.

"He knows about the Flemings and he knows about Carolyn," I said as soon as Fred got in. "He could be the one who killed her."

He started the engine and turned on the air. "We definitely made him nervous, and it had nothing to do with mold. I'll dig deeper and see what I can find."

"And I'll have lunch with my mom."

Fred backed out of his parking space and looked at me. "Okay. Did I miss the change of subject?"

"My mom and her friends are well acquainted with cosmetic surgeons. I'll see if she knows anything about this guy—where he lives, how he treats his wife and kids. Maybe she's even used him." That was a creepy thought. Maybe my mother had kissed my cheek with lips sculpted by a murderer.

Fred put the car into gear and pulled slowly out of the lot, merging into traffic. "Quite a sacrifice for you to make. What if she doesn't know anything?"

I shrugged. "I'll have an expensive lunch she'll pay for and for a few days she'll quit nagging me to come to see her. It's pretty much a win-win situation."

પ્

I got home in time to call my mother and set up a lunch for Sunday, shower again, change into cutoffs, and make a fresh batch of chocolate chip cookies before Trent arrived with a pizza. I'm not all that fast, but he was late. I'm not complaining since I'm usually the one who runs late, so it works out well if we both are.

Henry greeted Trent by winding around one of his legs then disappearing out the open door behind him. He had things to do and mice to meet.

I gave Trent a kiss and took the pizza box. "I made cookies."

"I can smell them."

We went into the kitchen and I got two cold Cokes while Trent took down the paper plates.

Usually Trent doesn't talk much about his work. *I can't discuss an ongoing case,* blah, blah, blah. While that is definitely not a bonding experience, it does mean I get to do most of the talking and I really enjoy talking.

We sat down at the table and I helped myself to a slice of double pepperoni pizza. "How was your day?" I was just being polite. I really wanted to tell him about my day, about Paula and Matthew and Dr. Jamison.

He swallowed and wiped his hands on a paper towel, my version of napkins. His gaze was intense, not a lot of green sparks in his dark eyes. I wasn't sure I wanted to hear what he had to say. "You got my curiosity up about your new neighbor, so in my spare time, I did a little checking and came up with some interesting details."

I set my pizza down and beamed at him. "You did that for me? That is so romantic!" I leaned over and gave him a greasy peck on the cheek. "Tell me."

He wiped the grease off his cheek and lifted his hands in a gesture of protest. "Don't get excited. It's all circumstantial, nothing that would seem significant if you hadn't told me about Sophie seeing her friend killed."

He didn't refer to Carolyn as Sophie's imaginary friend. That was a good start. "Go on."

"Did Sophie give you any idea why her family moved to Nebraska when she was five?"

"No. I thought you were going to give me information, not ask me questions." I took another bite of pizza, unimpressed so far with Trent's revelations.

"Be patient. I'm getting there."

If I had a quarter for every time I've been told to *be patient*, I'd have enough quarters to get my Cokes from vending machines for the rest of my life. "I'm the lady who gets speeding tickets while pulling out of my own driveway. What makes you think I have the ability to *be patient*?"

"Point taken. Okay, Robert Fleming was a business analyst with a local company here in Kansas City. One promotion, good prospects for another. Jan was a stay-at-home mom, active in her local church. Story book family. Then one day Robert gave notice at work and they moved to Omaha. Less than a week later the parents died from a gas leak. Sophie was spending the night with her aunt or she'd have died too."

"I already knew all that. Sophie told me. It's sad, but it's not news. Old house. Defective gas heater. It happens." I selected another piece of pizza and tried to *be patient.*

"The house was old, but it was in good condition. The owners had everything checked before the Flemings moved in. But that's not the really strange part."

I waited patiently. Well, I pretended to be patient.

"Somebody deposited a hundred thousand dollars into the Flemings' bank account the day before Robert gave his notice at work."

I sucked in a deep breath and leaned back in my chair. That detail was worth waiting for. "I did not know that." Fred probably didn't know that. He'd been focusing on the residents of his house, not on Sophie's family. Maybe I'd be able to tell him something. I love it when that happens. "Any idea where that money came from?"

Trent shook his head. "Bank account in the Caymans. I don't have the time or the authority to track it further since I'm only doing this to satisfy my girlfriend's curiosity, not to solve a crime."

"Blood money," I said. "Somebody paid Sophie's father to kill her best friend. No wonder Sophie's freaked out. Her father's a murderer."

Trent smiled and shook his head. "You've been watching too many episodes of *Castle*. Not only is that a major leap in logic, but there's also one big problem with your theory. I checked the records for six months before and six months after the time when the Flemings moved to Nebraska. No reports of a little girl named Carolyn going missing. No unsolved homicide of a small girl with blond hair."

I sighed and took a long drink of Coke. "Yeah, that seems to be the major stumbling block. Even Fred can't find any evidence Carolyn ever existed."

I probably shouldn't have said *even Fred*. Trent's eyes narrowed. The two of them are friends in a distant, removed sort of way. Well, maybe not *friends* so much as *friendly*. Connected through me. Trent's not always comfortable with how Fred does things, especially when he has no idea how Fred does things. But he can speculate, and he's pretty sure Fred doesn't always go through proper channels. Again with the overly moral stuff.

"We talked to the guy who owned Fred's house," I said. "He says it sat vacant for the five years he owned it." I told him about Dr. Daniel Jamison and his reactions when I mentioned Sophie's family and Carolyn. "We don't believe him. He's a doctor, a plastic surgeon, so he has money now. But he said he was in medical school during that time, and med students are usually broke. You think he could have got a student loan big enough to pay for a murder? No, probably not." I stuffed another piece of pizza into my mouth to keep it from saying something else silly.

Trent smiled. Most of the time he looks fierce and intimidating. A job requirement. But when he smiles, he looks like a mischievous little boy. I always kind of melt when he does that. "You seem to be forgetting the big glitch in your theory. We have no proof anybody was murdered."

I grinned. I couldn't help it in the presence of that smile even though we were talking about murder. "You know what your problem is, Detective Adam Trent? You get hung up on the tiniest little details."

He laughed. I laughed. We ate more pizza.

అ≪

I was sleeping peacefully with Trent's arms wrapped around me when Henry leapt off the bed and charged over to the window, growling deep in his throat.

"I thought you said Rick was in Hawaii," Trent mumbled sleepily, his breath warm on my neck.

I looked at the clock. Just after two a.m. "It's only Sophie making her nightly trek to Fred's house. Go back to sleep."

Apparently Henry thought I was talking to him. He leapt back onto the foot of the bed, yawned and closed his eyes.

But Trent was awake. "I've got to see this." He rose and strode over to the window, giving me a really nice view of his really nice butt in the moonlight.

"You're right," he said, his attention focused on the street. "She looks like a ghost, gliding across the street in that white gown. Fred must have been expecting her. He opened the door as soon as she walked onto the porch. She's going inside. Fred, you dog! Oh, they're both coming out again. He's walking her to her house." He turned around and headed back to bed. "You're right. That's downright creepy. That woman has definitely had some trauma in her life."

I opened my arms to him. "So have I. My boyfriend just left me in the middle of the night to watch another woman. He's going to have to figure out a way to make me feel wanted again."

Trent smiled and settled into bed beside me. "I accept the challenge."

Things were just getting interesting when Henry suddenly made a jungle-cat noise, shot out of bed and over to the window and continued to snarl.

Trent stopped what he was doing. Damn. "Sophie again?"

"No, he doesn't snarl at her. Maybe it's the white car again."

"The white car? What white car?"

My front doorbell rang.

Chapter Eight

Trent sat bolt upright and frowned. "You're sure Rick's in Hawaii?"

I shrugged. "I'm never sure of anything where he's concerned. He said he was going, but he hasn't sent me any pictures of the ocean and palm trees."

"Stay here." Trent was out of bed, into his blue jeans and out the door with gun in hand before I got my jeans zipped. If my jeans are ever loose enough I can zip them easily, I buy a smaller size.

Henry made it downstairs first with Trent close behind. I was halfway down when he reached the door and flung it open while holding the gun behind his back. "What do you—what the devil?"

Henry arched his back and hissed.

The devil was at my front door in the middle of the night? I should have listened to my mother and gone to church more often.

Trent shoved his gun into his waistband and opened the screen door. He was inviting the devil inside? That might be taking the whole manners thing a little far. I hoped he didn't expect me to serve him a Coke.

Henry gave a final snarl and darted outside. My cat deserted me.

At least Trent stood his ground. "What are you doing here?" he asked.

"Help me." A small thin form with big sad eyes and a bulging canvas bag inched his way into my house.

Rickie. I might have been better off if it had been the devil.

Trent looked back at me helplessly.

"Rickie, what are you doing here?" I peered around the boy, trying to see if Rick's car was outside. "Where's your father? Did he bring you over here?" I would chase him down and drag his sorry butt back if I had to swim all the way to Hawaii.

"Daddy and that woman left me all alone and I'm running out of food."

I looked more closely at the kid. The first time I saw him he reminded me of an orphan from a Dickens' novel. Once again he had that same *More, please,* look.

I reminded myself that he was not an orphan. He possessed not only the requisite two parents, but also one new stepfather and one visiting, temporary, pseudo stepmother. Well, calling Ginger a stepmother of any description might be something of an exaggeration, but I was pretty sure about the *visiting, temporary* and *pseudo* parts.

"They left you alone?" Trent asked, and I was surprised at the shock and horror in the big bad cop's voice. Wasn't he supposed to be more suspicious of people?

Rickie nodded.

"When? When did they leave?"

Rickie lifted his thin shoulders. "I dunno. When I got up Thursday morning, they were gone."

Trent looked at me and I shrugged. I could see Rick doing that. His own mother had probably done it to him when he was growing up. Marissa wouldn't win any Mother of the Year awards. On the other hand, I didn't trust Rickie either. He'd doubtless learned deceit before he learned his ABCs. Yet, there he was, alone on my front porch in the middle of the night.

"How did you get here?" I asked.

"I walked. It's a long way. I'm hungry. Have you got anything to eat?"

Trent dragged a hand through his hair, sighed and closed the door behind Rickie. "We've got some leftover pizza."

"I like pizza." He did the soulful eyes thing again.

In the months before my divorce from Rickhead was final, I had many fantasies of the nights I would spend with Trent once I was a free woman. Not a single one of those fantasies included warming up pizza at three in the morning for my ex-husband's runaway son. But I couldn't very well send him back out into the night.

Rickie followed Trent and me into the kitchen and sat down at the table. "You got any more cookies? I like cookies. And a Coke."

I took two pieces of the leftover pizza from the refrigerator and popped them into the microwave.

While they heated, I called Rick's cell phone. Of course it went straight to voice mail. I wasn't sure if he was out of range in Hawaii or had just turned his phone off. I left a message about his son, but I had very little hope he'd call me back even if he got the message.

"Go on home," I said to Trent. "Get some sleep. I'll take care of this." I inclined my head toward the seated boy.

"Not a chance." He opened the refrigerator door and reached inside. "I don't believe it. You actually have milk in here."

"For dunking Oreos and making hot chocolate. Duh."

He poured a glass of milk and set it in front of Rickie. The boy frowned and looked affronted. "I want a Coke."

"Yeah, well, I wanted to sleep another four hours this morning. We don't always get what we want. Lindsay, would you make me a cup of coffee?"

That probably sounds like an outrageous request since I've already admitted I don't drink and can't make coffee. But I can put a cup of water in the microwave for a minute then add a coffee bag.

After we got Rickie settled at the table with pizza and a glass of milk—no, that combination doesn't sound very good to me, either—Trent and I took our coffee and Coke and went from the brightly lighted kitchen to the dark living room.

I turned on a lamp, just one. I wasn't ready to deal with bright light. "What am I going to do with him? I've got to go to work in a few hours."

Trent sank onto the sofa with a long sigh. "Just when I thought we were finished with your ex."

I sat down beside him. "Thank goodness your ex is long gone." I recalled the story he'd told me when we'd first met. *We got married, we lived together for three years, then we got a divorce and stopped living together. Well, actually it was the other way around. We stopped living together and then got a divorce.*

He flinched and it seemed that a shadow flitted across his features, but it was hard to tell since the room was dark except for that one lamp. I was probably being paranoid. Not everybody's ex is a nut job like mine.

"I'll take Rickie home with me and contact social services," he said quietly.

It was my turn to flinch. "Foster care? The system?"

Trent shrugged, took a sip of his coffee and made a face. He'd have made a worse face if I'd brewed it from scratch. "I don't see anything else we can do. Grace and Rick have both abandoned the boy."

"Will foster care take him permanently or temporarily?"

"I don't know. If Grace and her new husband come back and show the court a stable home environment, she can probably get him back."

"No!" The boy in question appeared like a ghost out of the gloom. He clutched a half-eaten piece of pizza in one hand and a Coke in the other. I considered snatching that Coke away from him but opted to let it go under the circumstances. "You stole my daddy! Don't take away my mama too!"

No, I didn't steal Rick from Grace. I didn't even know about her until recently, but that was the story Grace told her son. It made a better story than the truth, and that whole family of con artists was big into *good stories*. Rickie was just carrying on the family tradition.

"Nobody's going to take your mother away," Trent said. "We're just trying to find a place where you can stay until your parents get back."

"I can stay in that room you've got upstairs where Mama and me stayed before. It doesn't have bugs. I liked staying there."

Rickie is not the sort of child that makes one want to rush right out and have unprotected sex, but I found myself feeling sorry for him. With Rick for a father, Grace for a mother and Marissa for a grandmother, it wasn't like the boy had any chance to be anything except obnoxious. Heredity and environment. Nature and nurture. All working toward the same end. If he had any chance at all, he didn't need to be thrown into the foster care system. Surely there was some other option.

"When's your mother coming back?"

"Lindsay, you're not thinking about—"

"Tomorrow," Rickie said, interrupting Trent's protest and moving closer to me. "It's just one more day. I knew you wouldn't let those people put me in a home where they'll beat me. I left a note on Daddy's door so when Mama comes to get me tomorrow she'll know where I am and she'll call you. I promise I won't be any trouble. You won't even know I'm here." He turned and went back to the kitchen.

Trent stood and started to go after Rickie then stopped and looked at me. "What just happened?"

I was only too familiar with that sort of happening. "Rickie's paternal genes are showing. He's learned how to close a deal…assume the answer is *yes* and proceed accordingly. I think he's coming into his own."

"I'll take him home with me then call social services."

That would certainly be the best idea. I really didn't want Rickie in my house for even one day, and I'd be surprised if he was telling the truth about his mother coming back in one day. "Take him with you, but don't call social services yet. Let me see if I can find one of Rick's friends to keep him."

"Rick has friends?"

"Okay, I'll look on Craig's List to see if I can find somebody to keep the kid."

Trent looked toward the kitchen where Rickie sat at the table, finishing his pizza and Coke. The glass of milk sat untasted. "Are you sure?"

My doorbell rang. For an instant I actually had a fleeting hope that it would be Grace or Rick coming to retrieve Rickie. Silly me.

Sophie stood on my front porch, shivering in the eighty degree temperature and looking terrified but wide awake. This time she was wearing a robe over her white nightgown. The robe was white too.

"I hope I didn't wake you," she said. "I saw your light was on."

"Come in." I stepped back so she could enter. "We were just having pizza with Coke and coffee.

Please join us." When the party's already underway, what's one more guest?

Henry darted past her, through the living room and into the kitchen. Perhaps he was going to attack Rickie.

She stepped inside then stopped. "Oh, you have company!"

"Yes, Sophie Fleming, this is Adam Trent, my..." Suddenly *boyfriend* seemed a little juvenile. My man? My significant other? My overnight guest? My lover? He was the man who made me happy. That was enough for me. There was no need to put a label on it.

Trent stepped forward and extended his hand. "Pleased to meet you, Sophie. Lindsay told me you did great things with that house across the street."

"This damn cat's got a mouse!" Rickie called.

"Would you excuse me a minute, Sophie?" I marched into the kitchen, opened the back door and looked at Henry. "You know you're not allowed to bring your friends inside."

Henry glared at me but carried the mouse outside.

I turned on Rickie. "When you were here before, you almost ruined my grandmother's sewing machine, you broke two glasses and one lamp, you spilled Coke on my sofa and you tore my shower curtain." I threw my hands in the air. "You are a walking disaster. I can deal with that, but you need to get one thing straight if you hope to spend one more minute in this house. You *will* treat my cat with respect."

He shrugged, looked down at the table and took another sip of Coke. The glass of milk and an empty Coke can sat on the table beside his empty pizza plate. "Whatever."

Some other time I'd point out to him the difference between *whatever* and *yes, ma'am*. At that moment I needed to get back to Trent and Sophie and see what had brought her to my door in the middle of the night.

Actually, it was getting to be early morning.

Whatever.

I grabbed a couple of Cokes before Rickie drank them all and returned to the living room to find Trent sitting on one end of the sofa looking confused and Sophie hovering on the other end still looking terrified.

I sat down between them, opened both Cokes and handed one to Sophie. That actually brought a tentative smile to her face.

"Thank you. Fred told me about your Coke habit."

"Fred can be a blabbermouth sometimes."

She tilted the can to her mouth and took a sip. "It actually tastes pretty good right now."

A convert.

"What's wrong, Sophie? Did you have another nightmare?"

She clutched the can of soda in both hands and bit her lip. "This time it wasn't a dream." She looked uncertain. "At least, I don't think it was."

I braced myself to hear about another murder. "Tell me."

She focused her gaze on Trent.

"It's okay," I assured her. "You can trust him. He's a cop."

She gasped, and her eyes widened.

Maybe somebody who dreamed about murder didn't want to tell a cop about it. "But he's not on duty," I added hastily.

Trent stood. "I think I'll go to the kitchen with Rickie and make myself some more coffee. Kid's probably ready for another glass of milk by now." He grinned at his own joke then left the room.

Sophie leaned closer. "She called me," she whispered.

"Who called you?"

"Carolyn. She—someone—said I killed her and if I didn't go back to Nebraska immediately, she was going to kill me."

"Wait a minute. If you killed her, she's dead. I'm pretty sure they don't get to make long distance phone calls from the hereafter. Are you sure you weren't dreaming?"

Sophie dropped her gaze and shook her head slowly. "When it happened, I was sure somebody had called me. I had the phone in my hand. I hung it up and looked out my window." She bit her lip. "I halfway expected somebody to be there. But now, I don't know. I had been walking in my sleep again, over to Fred's. He woke me and took me home. I was almost asleep when the phone rang."

"So maybe you were asleep and dreamed the phone rang."

Sophie lowered her head into her hands. "You must think I'm crazy."

I rejected several possible answers like *kind of* and *a little* and decided on, "You're under a lot of stress with the move back here and getting your business going."

She looked up and gave a half-hearted smile. "That's a very kind way of saying you think I'm crazy."

I laughed. "You're actually kind of an amateur at this *crazy* business. You've never met my former in-laws."

"You're right. I must have been dreaming. I'm so sorry I bothered you." She stood and smoothed her robe. "I'm going to go home now and try to stay there for a while."

"Not for long. Don't forget the party at my place tomorrow. I mean, tonight."

"I'll be here wearing normal clothes and trying my best to sound sane."

"Don't try too hard. You'll stand out."

As soon as the door closed behind her, Trent and Rickie came back into the living room. Trent had a firm grasp on Rickie's arm.

"What was that all about?" he asked.

"No big deal." I told him about the phone call that might or might not have been a real call but was not likely from a dead person. "Now she thinks she murdered a kid who didn't exist." I looked at Rickie. "Be warned. That's what happens to kids who insult my cat."

He shrugged. "Whatever."

I was getting really tired of that word really fast.

Chapter Nine

Saturday was a short workday…thank goodness. I got home in time to take a brief nap before everybody arrived. I had planned to do a bit of housecleaning, but decided a hostess with her eyes open was more important than a clean house.

Paula came over early to help me get ready. She was still pretending to be a little put out with me for inviting Matthew, but I could tell she was secretly pleased. Well, I hoped she was secretly pleased.

My back yard is protected from the sun by large trees and bushes, so even in the August heat, it wasn't completely unbearable. However, after spending my days in the kitchen at Death by Chocolate where at least a couple of ovens are always going, I probably gauge heat differently than most people. In deference to everybody else, I set a box fan on one side of the patio to move the torpid air around.

I knew the exact moment Trent and Rickie arrived. Paula was inside making iced tea and I was outside cleaning spiders, leaves and dust off the chairs on the patio when Zach and Henry ran out the back door making noises of protest. Henry was grumbling under his breath and Zach was shouting, "Anlinny! Anlinny!"

Henry darted off into the bushes and Zach closed the door firmly behind himself before he ran down the three back steps and over to me. "That boy that broke my green truck is here!"

I leaned down and brushed the soft hair off his concerned forehead. "If he breaks any more of your toys, I'll break his face."

"Okay. I'll go tell him." He started up the steps, but the screen door flew open, barely missing him as he scuttled back down the steps and over to my side.

Rickie strolled out clutching a Coke in one hand. That boy had a Coke problem. "Hi, Aunt Lindsay. Uncle Adam said I need to come out and help you."

Aunt Lindsay? Uncle Adam?

"Yeah, sure, why don't you clean off the grill?"

He walked over to the grill and stood beside it, looking blank.

"First you lift the lid." I performed the action. "Then you take this brush." I removed the metal brush from its holder on the side. "And you scrub the grill on both sides until it's clean and shiny instead of black and gunky."

"Why? You're just gonna cook on it and it's gonna get dirty again."

I snatched his Coke away from him. "You want a reason why? Because you don't get the soda back until that grill is clean and shiny."

He took the brush and began to move it back and forth across the grill in a lackadaisical manner. At that rate we wouldn't be ready to cook the burgers and brats before Labor Day, but maybe the activity would keep him out of trouble for a while.

Trent came out and took in the scene. "Hey, Zach, I think your mother needs your help in the house."

"Okay." Zach scurried past Rickie, giving the boy plenty of space, but on the top step he turned back. "If you break my toys, Anlinny's going to break your face."

Rickie shrugged. "Whatever." He kept brushing at the grill. It was probably one of the more benign threats he'd heard in his short lifetime.

Trent looked at me.

I returned his gaze. "Hey, I never claimed to have any maternal instincts."

He came over and gave me a quick peck of a kiss. In deference to the heat he was wearing shorts and a tank top. He has really nice, muscular legs. And arms. And chest. I'd have liked more than a peck, but that wasn't going to happen with Rickie around. How did couples ever manage to have a second child?

"Did you two have fun today?" I asked.

"Oh, yeah. Lots of fun. I took him to the zoo but they made me bring him back. Didn't have a cage strong enough to hold him. Did you find anybody?" He tilted his head in Rickie's direction. *Anybody who'd take care of the kid until his parents got back.*

I shook my head. "I have no idea where to start."

"You could have asked me." I turned at the sound of Fred's voice. He was making his way through the bushes with a picnic basket on each arm.

"I suppose I could have," I replied. "Okay, where would you suggest I start?"

"I said you could ask me. I didn't say I had any answers." He set his picnic baskets on the table and

95

opened them to reveal three bottles of wine in one and six wine glasses in the other. "I brought the cheap crystal in case things get ugly."

I cringed at his words. This was supposed to be a happy get together of friends, a *welcome to the neighborhood* event for Sophie and a *get to know Matthew* event for Paula with lots of fun and laughter and chocolate. However, the gathering did hold a few possibilities for violence. Rickie, who had a talent for making people want to kill him. Sophie who thought she might be a murderer. And, of course, Paula who might decide to kill me if Matthew turned out to be a jerk. I could only hope I had enough chocolate to keep everybody mellow. I had made something called Suicide by Chocolate especially for the party. With chocolate chip cookie dough, Oreo cookies, brownies, ice cream, chocolate syrup and caramel syrup, it should keep people smiling.

The back door opened again and Zach charged out waving a half-eaten brownie in one hand. Paula caught the door with her foot and emerged carrying a tray of condiments. She was smiling. Matthew was behind her with a pitcher of tea. He was smiling too. Fred's wine glasses appeared safe so far.

Zach made a wide circle around the grill where Rickie stood and ran over to greet Fred. "We got more brownies in the house." He waved his prize around and left a chocolate stain on the crease in Fred's left pants leg. "You can have some."

"Thank you." Fred barely flinched. Being around Zach is good for Fred. It has either taught him a degree of tolerance or given him the ability to hide his stress. Either one is a good thing.

Trent checked Rickie's progress on the grill. "Good job. We can burn off the rest of it. Do you want to help me start the fire?"

"Whatever." That word again. Maybe I could have it tattooed on his forehead then smack him upside the head every time he said it.

"Look what I found."

I turned at the sound of Zach's voice. He was holding out a small grubby hand for Paula and Matthew to see the long legged spider he'd captured.

Paula flinched but remained calm. A mom thing. It wasn't the first spider she'd seen, and even I recognized it as a harmless daddy longlegs. "That's nice," she said. "Put him down and go wash your hands."

"No! I'm going to keep him for Henry. He likes to play with spiders."

"That spider has a family, you know," Matthew said softly. "He's got a mother and father and brother and sister, and they're going to be worried about him if he doesn't come home."

Concern filled Zach's blue eyes as he looked at Matthew then at the spider which had recovered from shock and was crawling up his arm. "Did your brother go away and never come home and make everybody sad?"

It was a silly question, the kind of question little kids ask, but for an instant Matthew's face tensed and his eyes darkened as if the question had meaning for him, struck a painful nerve. He recovered almost immediately and the smile returned. "No, none of my brothers ran away from home, but I'd have been very upset if one of them had."

Zach nodded, accepting the answer. He went to the edge of the patio and carefully settled the creature back into the grass then returned to show Matthew his empty hands.

"Good job! You've just made that spider's family very happy. Now go wash those spider tracks off your hands so you can get ready to eat a hamburger."

Zach looked carefully at his hands. "Oh, yeah, spider tracks!" He ran up the steps and back into the house.

"You're good with him." Paula sounded a little surprised but pleased.

He looked at her, his expression soft. "I love kids. I'm the youngest in a big family, and by the time I came along, I had nieces and nephews running around everywhere."

He loved kids. He was gazing at Paula adoringly. Two marks in the plus column. So far there weren't any marks in the negative column.

Fred came up beside me. "I poured you a glass of wine. Drink it and stop staring."

I took the glass and followed him to sit in a chair on the far side of the patio, maybe the chair that spider and his family had called home until a short time ago.

"Matthew seems really nice." I took a sip of wine. It was delicious, of course. "You didn't find anything bad about him."

"Which doesn't mean there's nothing bad out there. Paula knows she has to be careful."

"Stop being such a cynic." I wondered if his cynicism extended to his nightly visitor. "Sophie came to my house after she left yours. She dreamed she got a call from Carolyn accusing her of murder."

"There's no way to know for certain what the caller said, but she did get a twenty second phone call at 2:43 this morning from a prepaid cell phone."

Of course he knew about the phone call. He'd had all day to talk to Sophie. I wondered how much of that day he'd spent talking to her. Interesting. He'd never before shown any interest in a woman.

"Speaking of somebody who's good with kids, check out your boyfriend."

I looked at Trent and Rickie where they presided over the grill. They'd managed to get the fire going without burning down the house. With Rickie participating, a house fire was always a possibility.

"Slide the turner under the patty in the direction of the grill," Trent instructed. "If you go across the grill, you could tear off pieces of the meat." The scene was sweet, but nothing I wanted to contemplate in any depth. Trent and I were still early in our relationship, much too early to think in terms of a family. But that wasn't the worst part. I had a bad feeling about Rickie. I didn't trust him. Yet Trent seemed to think he could be a mentor, maybe save the kid. That could be disastrous.

The back door opened and Zach came out, smiling and showing his clean hands.

"Looks good!" Matthew said. "I don't see any spider tracks. Come get your hamburger bun ready."

Zach ran over to the table, and Paula handed him a plate and bun then leaned over and kissed the top of his head.

I looked back at Trent whose attention was focused on explaining the finer points of barbecue to Rickie, but Rickie was watching the little scene with Zach. As soon as he saw me watching him, his expression changed from wistful to angry and he turned his attention back to the meat on the grill. With a quick flip, he rolled a brat off the grill and onto the patio.

I couldn't decide if I felt sorry for him or wanted to smack him. Probably a little of both.

"Hello, Sophie," Fred said, rising to his feet.

I turned to see Sophie in a white sundress and white strappy sandals coming around the side of the house. She smiled and waved a hand with perfect nails and a ring with a single perfect diamond.

"Glad you could make it. Would you like a glass of wine?" Fred offered.

"I rang the doorbell, but nobody answered."

"We're all out here." I rose so she could sit next to Fred. "You're just in time. Looks like the meat will be done any minute. Grab some wine to fortify yourself and I'll introduce you to everybody."

Fred handed her a glass and she stood beside him.

"Everybody, this is my new neighbor, Sophie Fleming." When I finished the introductions, I noticed Matthew watching her intently. Was that the first mark in his negative column—looking at another woman? Of course, she was beautiful, and looking at a beautiful person was sort of like looking at beautiful artwork. If Simon Baker walked into my backyard, I'd probably stare at him for a very long time but it wouldn't mean anything except that he was nice to look at. I decided I shouldn't condemn Matthew for looking at a beautiful woman. If he didn't look too long.

Trent declared the burgers and brats done, and everybody moved around, smearing mustard on buns, adding pickles and ketchup, heaping their plates.

In an effort to make our newest guest feel comfortable, I took a seat beside her. That put me on one side and Fred on the other, people she knew. Okay, it also insulated her from Matthew, but that was just a coincidence.

Trent took a seat on my other side while Matthew remained close to Paula even though he continued to sneak glances at Sophie. At some point I might have to reconsider putting a mark in the negative column.

Everybody settled into the activity of eating. Even Rickie, seated in a chair on the far corner of the patio, seemed momentarily content as he opened a fresh Coke and dove into the two burgers, one brat, potato salad, baked beans and Cheetos heaped on his plate. I considered sneaking something into his food that would mellow him out for a few hours, but of course I didn't. If I'd had something like that I'd have taken it myself.

Everybody ate, everybody talked and everybody laughed. True to his word, Matthew brought a wonderful watermelon, the best I'd tasted in years. When everyone was properly stuffed, we put the leftovers in the refrigerator, shoved the paper plates and napkins into a large trash can, then relaxed to give our food time to settle before we started on dessert.

The sun was getting low and the cool shadows of evening had begun to spread around our little party when Matthew strolled over to talk to Sophie. I had abandoned my chair in the business of cleaning up, and he took my place.

I moved a little closer and poured myself another glass of wine. Okay, I moved closer to hear what they were saying. It was a small patio, not like I had to go out of my way to eavesdrop.

They exchanged the usual polite jibber jabber about the good food and hot weather, and I was ready to move on to more interesting eavesdropping when he brought up the subject of her residence there as a child. "You left here when you were pretty young. You must have some really good memories of living here to want to come back."

It was an innocuous comment, certainly not flirtatious, but it got my attention because of the Carolyn thing. I lifted the glass of wine to my lips and pretended to be fascinated with the big oak tree on one side of my patio.

"You're not very good at being inconspicuous." Fred had sneaked up behind me. Not that he had to be very sneaky. I'd been too intent on listening to Matthew and Sophie to notice.

I gave him a quick glare then returned to studying the oak tree and sipping my wine. From the corner of my eye, I saw him pour more wine then move away, but not far. He was listening too.

"Yes," Sophie said. "That house contains a lot of good memories."

"How about the other houses around here? This one, the one next door? Did you have friends in the neighborhood?"

Again, the question was innocent enough, and I might not have noticed the tension in Matthew's voice if I'd been looking directly at him instead of at the tree. But I was focused only on his voice and I did hear the tension.

Sophie hesitated. "No," she finally said. "I didn't have friends. I don't remember friends. Just my family."

"Family's important. I can understand why you'd want to reconnect."

A hand clutched my shoulder. I gasped and whirled around, expecting to see Sophie or Matthew and be forced to justify my eavesdropping.

Trent smiled and wrapped an arm about my waist. "Sorry. Didn't mean to startle you. You were really off in your own little world."

"Yeah, just thinking about, uh, things."

"Why don't you think about some chocolate dessert to complete this evening of gluttony?"

I grinned up at him. "I can do that."

Suicide by Chocolate was a huge success, and we all relaxed in a stupor as the shadows of evening settled around us.

Trent sat beside me and took my hand in his. There's something incredibly romantic about sitting under the stars in a lawn chair holding hands with somebody you care about. I could have sat there all night or at least until I went to sleep and my head dropped over and I woke with a horrible crick in my neck.

Paula was the first to announce she had to leave. Zach had fallen asleep in Matthew's lap. "I need to get home and put him to bed." She stood and reached for her son.

"I'll carry him," Matthew offered.

She didn't object, and the three of them set off through my yard toward her house. I watched them in the moonlight. It was a nice image, Zach with his head resting on Matthew's shoulder, Paula walking beside them. So what if Matthew had looked at Sophie a long time and asked her questions about the house? Since he had no knowledge of her problems, he couldn't have known those questions would sound suspicious to someone who happened to overhear.

Sophie stood. "Thank you so much for inviting me. I enjoyed meeting everyone, and the food was wonderful. As soon as I get everything settled in my house, we'll have to do this again at my place, provided you'll bring the dessert, Lindsay."

"I'll walk you home." Fred rose from his chair. "Lindsay, as always, it was wonderful."

The two of them strolled off toward the street. Trent, Rickie and I were left alone in the warm summer evening under a beautiful full moon. Could have been romantic. Wasn't.

"Grab those Coke cans," Trent instructed Rickie, "and Lindsay and I will get the rest."

I think the kid mumbled *whatever* under his breath, but he did pick up a couple of cans.

We stuffed the last of the party debris into the trash can and went inside.

"Okay, Rickie," I said, "you can have the bathroom first. I'm sure you'll want to shower after being outside in the heat all evening."

"Nah." He slumped on the sofa and turned on the TV.

Trent turned off the TV and yanked the remote away from him. "Yeah."

Rickie trudged up the stairs, grumbling under his breath.

Trent pulled me into his arms for a tantalizing, chocolate flavored kiss.

"You're going to leave me, aren't you?" I asked.

"I just don't feel right staying here with the kid in the house."

This was the man who refused to classify our relationship as more than friends or do more than kiss me until my long, drawn-out divorce from Rickhead was final. I wasn't surprised.

"Fine." I sighed. "We'll have to make up for it next weekend."

We walked out onto my front porch and did a little more kissing and cuddling. I wasn't going to make it easy for him to leave.

The soft closing of a door at Paula's house diverted my attention. I'd almost forgotten that Matthew had gone home with her and hadn't returned. Trent has that effect on me, makes me forget everything going on in the rest of the world. It's a nice feeling.

We were pretty much hidden on my porch by the dark and the trees, so I watched shamelessly.

The two of them stood on her porch, talking quietly, apparently comfortable with each other. Paula looked up at him and he looked down at her. They stood that way for a very long time. Good grief! Was I going to have to tell them when the time was right for a kiss?

He turned and walked off the porch and Paula went back inside.

"Damn!" I whispered.

"Hey, think of how long you and I knew each other before I got up the courage to kiss you."

"That was different. Paula's ex-husband is in prison. There's no reason they can't make out."

I watched Matthew walk to the street and get into his car. His white sedan. Like the white sedan I'd seen going slowly down the street.

I was being paranoid. White sedans were not exactly unusual.

"That's the car that parked up the street last night and the man watched that woman in white go to Fred's house."

I whirled around to see that Rickie had joined us.

I could tell by the smell that he had not taken a shower.

<u>Chapter Ten</u>

"How do you know that?" I demanded, not wanting to believe. "There are thousands of white cars in Kansas City."

"Nah," the kid said. "Not with that license plate."

"You remember the license plate?" Trent asked.

Rickie stared as the car drove away down the street. "Yeah. Mama says you gotta pay attention to anything suspicious. That guy sitting there in his car in the middle of the night was suspicious."

I was impressed he knew a three-syllable word like *suspicious*, but I was not convinced he was telling the truth.

"Tell me exactly what you saw." Trent sounded like a cop. Sometimes that's kind of hot. It wasn't at the moment.

Rickie shrugged. "Just that car parked up the street and that woman running over to Fred's house in her nightgown. I thought at first the guy in the car was watching me, but he left after Fred took the woman home." He turned to go back into the house.

I grabbed his shoulder. "Did you see Matthew in that car? Could you see good enough to identify him?"

He frowned up at me. "It was dark and the streetlight's broke." He shrugged off my hand and went inside. Immediately the sound of the TV

107

overpowered the soothing sounds of crickets and night birds.

Damn. I'd worked so hard to set up Paula and Matthew, and it had worked. She liked him. Zach liked him. But suddenly I wasn't so sure I'd done the right thing. Had that been him driving around in the middle of the night, spying on Sophie? He had looked at her for a long time at the barbecue. Was he obsessed with Sophie? Was he stalking her? Maybe he'd even come into the restaurant and hit on Paula because he knew she was Sophie's neighbor.

Maybe I was overreacting. It wouldn't be the first time.

"You think the kid was telling the truth?" Trent asked, breaking into my train of self-flagellation.

"I don't know. I have seen a white car driving slowly down the street in the middle of the night a couple of times."

"That would be the white car you mentioned before Rickie rang the doorbell and interrupted us?"

"Yes, that would be the same white car."

"So it's been coming around for a while and you didn't think maybe you should tell me about it?"

"If that car had a machine gun aimed out the passenger window or a leg hanging out of the trunk, I'd have told you. But a car driving down my street? No, I didn't see any reason to tell you."

Trent ran a hand through his hair. "You're right. It's just that so many strange things have happened to you. I worry about you."

I took the opportunity. "Given any more thought to teaching me to shoot and getting me a gun?"

He looked at me for a long moment as if he was actually thinking about my request. "No. Are you going to say something to Paula about what Rickie just told us?"

"I don't know. I don't know if there's anything to tell."

"Before you talk to her, I'll check out Matthew and let you know what I find."

I decided it would be best not to tell him Fred had already done that. Sometimes Fred's activities made him a little nervous. Besides, it wouldn't hurt to have a second opinion. "Thanks. How about taking care of my latest speeding ticket while you're in the system?"

"No."

Never hurts to ask.

We indulged in one final delicious kiss.

"Stay with me," I whispered.

"I can't. I'll make it up to you, I promise." He kissed me again. "Love you, babe." He turned and walked away.

What? *What?*

Had he just casually tossed out the *L* word?

No, surely I hadn't heard right.

He got in his car, waved and drove off.

I'd heard right.

Damn! He'd tossed it out there so casually, in a totally unintimidating manner. Maybe it had just slipped out and he didn't realize it.

No, that wasn't Trent. He realized what he'd said.

And now I had to make up my mind if I could say it back.

I swallowed and bit my lip.

If I ignored it, pretended it hadn't happened, he'd probably never bring it up again. He'd tossed the ball into my court and it was entirely up to me what I was going to do with it. Damn! I hate responsibility.

Not that I doubted how I felt about Trent. I just didn't want to think about it or analyze it or put it into words. I didn't want to face my feelings.

I turned to go back inside. I'd think about it later.

When I opened the door, Henry darted up to join me. Rickie lounged on my sofa, his gaze intent on the TV screen.

"Up to bed," I directed.

"I'm hungry. I want another cookie."

"You cannot possibly be hungry after everything you ate, and you're not getting another cookie. Up to bed now or..." I tried to think of something I could use to threaten him, something that would generate some action instead of a bored *whatever*. "I'll turn Henry loose on you."

Rickie glared at Henry. Henry lifted his tail and snarled.

"If I go to bed now, can I have a Coke for breakfast?"

"Yes." Like I could stop him.

He dragged himself upstairs into the guest room. I thought about demanding he shower first, but I didn't need another battle at that hour. I'd fumigate the room after he left.

I showered then peeked in to be sure he was actually in bed. He was.

"Good night, Aunt Lindsay."

I shuddered at the obvious scam attempt but responded politely. "Good night."

The last thing I did before going to bed was to call Fred and update him on the Matthew situation.

"Something's going on," he said. "Somebody's afraid of what Sophie knows. It could be Matthew. He could be the one who made that ridiculous call, pretending to be Carolyn and threatening her."

"That pretty much affirms that Carolyn was a real person, not just Sophie's imaginary friend."

"If we make that assumption, it could mean that Sophie actually witnessed her murder."

"So why did her parents tell her she imagined the whole thing? Do you think one of them was the murderer?"

He was silent for a long, telling moment. "Right now I have more questions than answers. I'll dig a little deeper and see what else I can find out about Matthew. At this point, he's our only lead."

With Trent and Fred both on Matthew's trail, we should soon know what he ate for breakfast and what kind of toilet paper he used.

I stretched out on my comfortable, cool bed and blessed the inventor of air conditioning. Henry stretched out at the foot of that bed, but he never seemed to mind the heat. I suspected he only blessed the inventor of the can opener.

I thought briefly about Trent's parting words then decided it wasn't the right time to think about it. I had too much else on my mind. I'd think about it tomorrow.

I was just drifting off to sleep when Henry's purr changed to a low growl. Damn. Sophie out for a stroll? A mysterious white car prowling around the neighborhood? I didn't want to deal with either one. I was tired. I just wanted to sleep.

Instead of darting to the window to peek out, Henry leapt out of bed and went to my bedroom door where he stood on his hind legs and slapped at the knob.

I swung my feet out of bed, heart rate accelerating. "You want out? You need to go to the bathroom?" He'd never done that, but I was really hoping for a little irritable bowel syndrome instead of a warning that somebody was in my house. We'd been that route before, and he'd been right. It's not a fun experience to discover uninvited guests in the middle of the night.

Henry growled and pawed the knob more determinedly.

My iron skillet was in the kitchen and I hadn't convinced Trent to get me a gun. I had no weapon.

Well, that wasn't totally true. I had a twenty-three pound ferocious cat.

I pushed him out of the way, opened the door and forced myself to step into the hallway.

There was someone in my house, but he wasn't coming upstairs. He was at the front door trying to get out.

"Rickie!"

The boy's thin shoulders flinched in his faded Batman pajamas. He turned and looked up. "I was hungry."

"Really? And you thought there was food in the front yard? Or maybe you were planning to drive to the closest fast food place. Oh, wait, you don't have a driver's license or a car."

He shrugged and started back upstairs. "I was bored," he mumbled. "There's not even a TV in that room."

"That's because you're supposed to sleep in that room!"

Henry gave a disgusted snort and stalked back to our room.

Rickie trudged dejectedly back to his room. He crawled into bed with a long sigh, glared at me and pulled the sheet over his head.

"I'm locking the door. If you need to go to the bathroom, knock on the wall and I'll let you out."

I closed the door and stepped into the hallway. I couldn't lock the door. I didn't even have the key to it. I could only hope he'd buy into my bluff.

☜☞

The next morning at breakfast (yes, I let Rickie have his Coke) I asked the kid when his mother was due back in town.

He looked down at the table top and shrugged. "I dunno."

"She's not coming back today, is she?"

Another shrug. "I dunno."

I wasn't surprised. I'd once been married to his father. I knew the odds of anything either of them said being true...about the same as the odds of winning the progressive jackpot on a slot machine. It happens. Just not on a regular basis.

"I'm meeting my mother for lunch today," I said.

He scraped the last bite of scrambled egg off his plate, ate it and shrugged again. "Whatever."

113

"We need to decide where you're going to stay while I'm gone."

"I'll stay here."

I gave a very fleeting thought to that possibility. Lock him in the basement, chain him to the wall...but I didn't have any chains. "You're nine years old. You're too young to stay by yourself."

He rolled his eyes. "Mama lets me stay by myself all the time."

"Well, I'm not your mother, and you're not staying here by yourself. I could ask Paula to babysit you—"

He slammed his Coke can down on the table and glared at me. "I'm not a baby. I don't need a babysitter."

"Okay, then you could go to Paula's and stay with her for the couple of hours I'll be gone."

"Whatever."

"Or you could go over to Fred's house."

He shuddered. "I don't want to stay with him."

"Fred's place it is."

"Oh, man!"

When I called Fred to tell him the plan, he was almost as thrilled as Rickie. "I'll lock up the silver and get out my bullet-proof vest."

It would be a character-building experience for both of them.

And if painful experiences built character, I'd be getting some character at lunch. I surveyed my wardrobe then chose the gray silk blouse and matching slacks my mother gave me for Christmas. Next I plugged in my flat iron to straighten my hair. I wanted to talk about Daniel Jamison, not my appearance, so I went all out.

When I came downstairs wearing the gray silk, makeup, straight hair and heels, Rickie had the volume on the TV turned up so high my mini blinds were shimmying.

"Heads up," I shouted. "Turn off the television and let's go."

He sighed and hit the kill button. The sudden silence was abrupt and beautiful. He stood and stared at me then frowned. "You look nice."

"Why, thank you, Rickie."

"You look like you got money."

Oh, so that's what *nice* meant in Rickie's world. I should have known.

I walked him over to Fred's house and rang the doorbell. "There's an extra Coke waiting for you if you behave yourself while I'm gone. Don't break anything and don't spill anything."

"Big deal. You got plenty of Cokes."

"I'll make fresh cookies."

Fred opened the door before Rickie could respond to that bribe. "Come in, Rickie, and have a seat on the sofa. I'll be right with you."

Rickie's upper lip curled in a sneer, but he moved past Fred into the house without a protest.

Fred held a sheet of paper toward me. "I made a list of some things you need to ask your mother about Dr. Jamison."

"Really? After all this time, you don't think I can conduct an interview with my own mother?" I snatched the paper from him and glanced at the orderly printed list. "I believe I can handle this."

"I'm not disputing your ability to handle this one alone, but I wish I could be there."

"Trust me, you don't." I hadn't given it much thought, but this would be my first time to put on a disguise and go out alone to try to elicit information from somebody even though that somebody was my mother.

"Call if you get in trouble."

"It's my mother."

"I realize that. Get back as soon as you can." Fred looked over his shoulder. I followed his gaze. I couldn't see Rickie, but I could see the sofa and he wasn't sitting on it.

"Don't kill him while I'm gone." I turned to go then looked back. "But if you do, I'll help you hide the body."

Fred actually smiled.

I walked off his porch and across my yard, careful to avoid tripping in those heels. This was the first time I wasn't looking forward to dragging information out of someone. But, what the heck, we were going to one of the best restaurants in Kansas City. The food would be good.

Henry met me halfway across the yard and looked up inquiringly.

"I'm sorry," I said. "He's not gone for good. He's only staying with Fred until I get home. But I'll give you some catnip tonight so you can get through it."

He flipped his tail into the air and stalked off.

≈≈

My mother was waiting when I got to the restaurant. We exchanged air kisses.

"You look very nice," she said. I didn't think she meant it the same way Rickie had. Or maybe she did.

"So do you, Mom." She did, in both definitions of the word. She wore a soft blue dress that accented her assets. I inherited my aerodynamic form from my mother, but she had so many modifications made, the resemblance was no longer apparent. Her chin length blond hair swung sleek and straight, and I knew for a fact it didn't grow out of her head with either of those attributes.

The hostess seated us at a table by a window so we could look out onto the green lawn and small lake. I don't serve atmosphere at my restaurant. It has no discernible flavor. Nevertheless, I found the view quite pleasant, and after a couple of sips of wine, I started to relax.

While we ate our salads, Mother updated me on all the people I didn't care about getting updates on. "Maribeth Carson came to the Fundraiser for Drought-Stricken Farmers wearing the very same red dress she wore to the Fundraiser for the Orphans in Africa. She might have got away with it if the dress had been black, but it was bright red. But that wasn't the worst part. Mark Hardesty showed up with that tramp he dumped Roxanne for, and she's pregnant. He has grandkids older than that child will be." Blah, blah, blah, blah.

When our grilled tilapia entrees arrived, I decided it was time to launch into grilling my mother.

"I have a friend who's thinking of getting some cosmetic work done. Do you know anything about Daniel Jamison?"

Mother paused, a bite of fish on her fork. She arched one perfect eyebrow and smiled. "Daniel is good, but there are others I'd recommend. Lindsay, you won't regret this decision. You don't need much. I think just a little around the eyes, and that chin you inherited from your father could use some tightening."

I almost choked. I started to protest but decided if I let her assume I intended to do something, I might get more answers. "So he's good, but not the best? He has a really nice office. Looks like he's doing well."

Mother's eyes lit up, and I could tell I was going to get a juicy piece of gossip. "Daniel is good, but his heart's just not in it. When Natalie married him, he wanted to be a general practitioner and heal the world. But he was on a scholarship. His family is dirt poor. Natalie decided she wasn't going to be married to just an ordinary doctor and she holds the purse strings, so he went into the specialty she chose for him."

I lifted an eyebrow in amazement. "One of your circle of friends married a guy with no money?"

Mother and folded her hands, highlighting her perfectly manicured nails. "Natalie's not exactly a friend. She's a couple of years older than me, but I remember the story quite well. Just before a big homecoming dance, her fiancé dumped her and married a waitress." If she'd said *prostitute* instead of *waitress*, she couldn't have said it with more disdain. Since I wanted something from her, I refrained from reminding her that her daughter was a waitress. "I don't think Natalie cared that much about her fiancé," she continued, "but she was totally humiliated. It was quite a scandal."

Mother lifted her glass and took a dainty sip of wine. She looked pleased. I had no problem believing Natalie was *not exactly* her friend.

"Of course she needed an immediate replacement. Daniel was very good looking and any girl would have been thrilled to go out with him even though he was on a scholarship and came from some religious farm where everybody's poor and they wear ugly clothes."

That was an interesting coincidence. Fred had told me Matthew came from Seventh Gate, the religious farm community west of town.

"Daniel was very nice and very shy and didn't seem to have any idea half the women at the university were interested in him. He was completely focused on his studies." Mother paused while the waiter refilled her wine glass. "When Natalie went after him, Daniel never stood a chance."

Mother seemed to like Daniel Jamison in spite of his humble beginnings. I wondered if she had been one of the women interested in him before Natalie stepped in. "Did you know he owned Fred's house for a while? Apparently he and his wife were having problems and he considered moving out."

Mother ate a bite of fish and looked pleased. "Of course Natalie never mentioned it, but I'm not surprised. It was probably when one of Daniel's

119

younger brothers moved in with them. They'd only been married a couple of years and he was still in medical school, but he wanted to help his brother go to college. I think he had about a dozen brothers and sisters. Honestly, those people have never heard of birth control."

A younger brother? Matthew was younger than Daniel. Was he the plastic man's brother? Had Dr. Dan lied about nobody living in Fred's house? It seemed awfully suspicious that the house would have sat empty for five years. Had Matthew lived there, been somehow connected with Sophie? I gulped the rest of my wine.

"Natalie didn't like having him there," Mother continued, oblivious to my approaching breakdown. "Usually Daniel did whatever she told him to do, but he stood his ground on that one. Maybe they bought the house for the brother to live in though I don't think he ever moved there because Natalie complained incessantly about how he was always underfoot and how much money they spent on him."

Sophie had mentioned Carolyn and her mother, nothing about a boy. Upon reflection, I doubted the brother had lived in that house but I was still bothered by the possible connection between Matthew and Daniel. "Do you remember the brother's name?" I held my breath.

"The whole family had Bible names."

Bible names? Like *Matthew*? I coughed, grabbed for my glass of wine which had somehow become empty, then settled for a long drink of water.

Mother frowned, a peculiar expression since her forehead didn't move thanks to her latest round of Botox. "Did you find a bone in the fish? I'll get the waiter." She lifted a peremptory hand, but I shook my head.

"No. The fish is fine. What was the brother's name?"

"Lindsay, why are you so interested in Daniel's brother? Does this have something to do with your decision to have some work done? He's a little old for you, and I think he's still married to his third wife. Or maybe she's his fourth. Anyway, someone like Gregg Lansford would be more appropriate. You dated him in high school, remember? He just went through a divorce too so you have something in common."

"Mother, what is his name?"

She did the frown thing again. "I just told you. Gregg Lansford."

"No, what is Daniel's brother's name?"

"Oh, are we back to him again? He's Jay Jamison. I'm sure you've heard of him. He's an attorney but not in the same class as your father. Jay represents murderers and drug dealers and he's on television a lot. He loves the press. He even has an ad on television." From the tone of her voice, I envisioned Jay Jamison's ad featuring a prostitute in skimpy black leather, wielding a whip and gun in one hand, a crack pipe and heroin needle in the other with a banner running across the bottom showing Jay Jamison's name and phone number. *Need help? Call Jay Jamison.*

"Everybody's entitled to legal representation, blah, blah, blah. Mother, Jay's not a Biblical name. Is that maybe his middle name? Do you remember his name?"

"Let me see. Something old-fashioned, but those old-fashioned names are becoming trendy again." She tapped the table with one white-tipped fingernail. "Joshua. That's it. Natalie called him Jay, but Daniel always used the full name. Joshua."

I let out a long breath. Not Matthew. I still had some concerns about him, but I was glad to know he wasn't directly linked to the house where Sophie dreamed she saw someone die. Fixing Paula up with a stalker would be bad enough, but I was pretty sure she'd be extremely upset with me if he turned out to be a murderer.

<u>Chapter Eleven</u>

My first impulse when I got home after my lunch with Mom was to rush into my house, eat half a dozen brownies and relax for an hour or three or four before fetching Rickie. But I couldn't do that to Fred. Anyway, he'd know. Fred knows everything. I'm certain he has all the houses in the neighborhood bugged or he has x-ray vision or he's psychic. Maybe all three.

When Fred answered his door, I expected to see him disheveled and distressed, but he was immaculate and calm. He must have locked Rickie in the basement.

I entered the living room to find the boy sitting on the sofa with a book in his lap.

"Rickie, why don't you go outside while Lindsay and I talk?" Fred requested. "Don't leave the yard."

Without a protest, a shrug or a *whatever*, Rickie laid down the book and walked outside.

"What did you do to him?" I asked as soon as the door closed behind him. "Did you beat him? Drug him? You haven't had him long enough to brainwash him."

Fred shook his head. "Really, Lindsay, you come up with some of the strangest notions. We just had a little chat. Would you like wine or Coke?"

"Coke and chocolate if you have any. I had plenty of wine at the restaurant but no decent chocolate. They had chocolate mousse, but it was mediocre. I guess I'm spoiled by my own baking."

"Well, I suppose there's no reason to be humble when you're the best." He went to the kitchen and I sat down on the sofa.

I picked up the book Rickie had been holding. *The Shining* by Stephen King. If the kid had actually been reading it, I hoped it didn't give him any ideas for new mischief.

Fred returned with a brownie and Coke for me and a glass of wine for himself.

"You survived your mother and I survived your stepson," he said as he settled in his recliner.

I flinched. "I wish you wouldn't call him that. I'm not married to his father. He's not my stepson."

"Very well. Your ex-husband's son failed to destroy my house or my person in spite of his best efforts. Tell me what you learned about Daniel Jamison."

I repeated my mother's stories. "I didn't really learn anything useful, but the possible connection between him and Matthew is creepy. Can you find out anything else about those people out there?"

"It's difficult to find information about them because they're not in any of the public records."

"Does that mean we're going to pay them a visit?"

"Maybe. I've got a couple more things I want to try. Take your ex-husband's son home and let me get back to work."

I finished my Coke and set the can on the coffee table. "You're doing such a good job with him, I thought maybe you'd want to keep him for a while."

"Very funny. No word from his mother?"

"I haven't checked my land line messages, but I doubt it."

"What are you going to do with him while you work tomorrow?"

I heaved a deep, sincere sigh. "I don't know. Maybe I can leave him at Zach's babysitter."

"Only if you don't care if the woman never speaks to you again."

"I could stick him in one of the ovens at the restaurant. Shove something under the handle so he can't get out."

"I hope you have no plans to become a mother."

"You ever think about getting married? Having a family?" For all I knew, he could have been married five times and have a dozen offspring. That's how little I know about him.

"I've often thought about flying, but that doesn't mean I plan to find the nearest tall building and try it."

"Good decision. I tried it from our rooftop when I was five. Dropped like a rock."

I went outside and found Rickie sitting quietly on Fred's front steps. I looked back at Fred. "Are you sure you didn't drug him?"

He closed the door.

"Let's go home and eat some leftovers. I've got to work tomorrow so we have to go to bed early tonight."

"Okay."

It wasn't *yes, ma'am*, but it was better than *whatever*.

When we got home, he voluntarily took a shower. I sent up a short but fervent prayer that the effects of whatever Fred had done to him would last for a few days, at least until someone came to reclaim him.

∮

Henry woke me a little after two a.m., leaping onto my chest and yowling. Obviously the soothing effects of his catnip had worn off.

"If this is Sophie doing her nightly visitation thing again, you're cut off catnip for the rest of your natural life."

He leaped off the bed but instead of going to the window that looked out on the street, he went to the side window where he stood with his paws on the sill.

I went to the window and looked out at the trees that separated my house from Fred's. It was a beautiful moonlit night and a soft breeze stirred the leaves.

Then the leaves on a branch close to the house shuddered wildly. Considering everything that had been going on, that was a little creepy. "You better not be carrying on about a raccoon or a possum," I warned, though I was seriously hoping to see a pointy little face appear among the leaves. Better than the alternative.

That's sort of what happened. Rickie, dressed in T-shirt and shorts instead of pajamas, crawled out of the foliage and reached for the window sill of the guest room.

"Hey!" I shouted.

He fumbled and almost fell but grabbed the window at the last minute and pulled himself up, disappearing inside.

I charged out of my room and down the hall to the guest room door. Silly me, thinking I could control Rick's son by just telling him he was locked in a room. If there hadn't been a window, he'd have tunneled out from the second floor.

I yanked the door open and he fell into my arms.

"He's after me!" he shouted.

"Nobody's after you. You've just been busted and you're not getting out of it with some ridiculous story."

"Yes, he is after me! The man in Sophie's house. He saw me and he came after me!"

I disentangled myself from his arms and pushed him away so I could look into his eyes. He was doing a really good job of looking scared. Terrified, actually. "Sophie's house? Have you been at her house? What were you doing over there? Either you tell me the truth or I'll take you back to Fred's!"

"I am telling the truth! You made me to go to bed too early and you don't have television in here or anything, so I climbed out the window, and when Sophie went over to Fred's house, I went in her house."

"You broke into Sophie's house?"

"No! She left the back door open. I just went in. If the door's already open, why shouldn't I go in?"

I threw up my hands in frustration. I didn't believe Sophie left her door open, but I wasn't going to argue with him in the middle of the night. "You

127

don't go in somebody's house unless they invite you." I shook my head. "Go back to bed. We'll apologize to her tomorrow."

I turned away, but he grabbed my arm. "No! There was a man who came in after I did, and he went in the kitchen and did something to her stove and then he turned around and saw me and chased me!"

I studied him more closely. I hadn't turned on the hall light, but even in the moonlight I could see the perspiration on his brow. The fear in his eyes and his voice seemed genuine.

"What did he do to her stove?"

He stood on one foot and then the other. "I don't know. He did something behind it. I think he cut something. He had a knife. A big knife."

"What did the man look like?" If he said it was Matthew—well, if he did, I'd decide then whether or not to believe him.

He wiped a hand across his face. "He was huge and his face was covered with a black mask and he had a gun."

A knife and a gun. If I let him continue, the guy would soon acquire a grenade and a rocket launcher. "I'll tell you what we're going to do. We're going over to Sophie's house to check out her stove. We're going to wake her up in the middle of the night. If you're telling the truth, she'll be grateful to us. If you're not, you're in big trouble."

He staggered away from me. "No! I don't want to go back! What if that man's still there?"

"We'll take an iron skillet and Fred with us."

He looked to one side of the room and then the other as if searching for an escape route. I grabbed his arm just in case he headed for the window again.

I didn't believe Rickie. Not completely. But his attitude was so different from his normal surliness, I had to give him some credence.

I called Fred, grabbed my cell phone and my iron skillet, took Rickie by the hand and met Fred as we headed to Sophie's house. Rickie tugged, whined and protested the entire way.

As we crossed the street, I saw something sparkling lying on the pavement, something catching the moonlight and reflecting it back in a thousand facets.

Sophie's ring.

We stopped. Fred picked it up and looked at me. "It's hers," he said.

"She dropped it when she went back home!" Rickie said, struggling harder.

Fred shook his head. "She didn't have it on when she came to my house."

I had to focus to control the hand holding my iron skillet. "You stole her ring," I accused.

"That man must have dropped it," Rickie mumbled, looking down at the street.

"The truth." Fred stood directly in front of him. Since Rickie didn't look up, he couldn't have seen Fred's gaze, but I was sure he could feel it.

"It was just laying there on the table. I picked it up to look at it and then I saw that man and I ran away and forgot I had it and I guess I dropped it when I ran across the street because I was scared for my life and I wasn't paying attention."

"You'll give it back to her and apologize." Fred sounded angry. Very angry.

So was I, but I couldn't match the anger in Fred's voice. I couldn't recall ever hearing that tone coming from him before.

He put the ring in his pocket and we continued to Sophie's house.

Her front door was unlocked.

"I unlocked it," Rickie said, still looking down. "When I was trying to get away."

"Call her, Lindsay," Fred instructed. "I'm going in."

I released Rickie's hand, set my iron skillet on the porch and took my cell phone from my pocket. I heard Sophie's phone ringing inside the house just before I heard Fred shout, "Gas! Call 911 and go to the other side of the street!"

Gas? Someone had done something to her stove, maybe cut the gas line with a big knife, just as Rickie said. Maybe he hadn't lied.

But he had stolen her ring.

He had saved Sophie's life.

But he was a thief.

Chapter Twelve

"Go back inside my house!" I shoved Rickie toward the street, killed my call to Sophie and punched in 911. "Gas leak!" I shouted into the phone, then took a leap of faith in Rickie's story and added, "Home invasion!"

While I answered their questions, I grabbed my trusty iron skillet and ran around to the side of the house where the gas meter was located. I needed a wrench but all I had at the moment was the skillet. I used the handle to whack the lever in the direction to turn off the gas to the house. The gas company would probably be upset with me for damaging their equipment. They could get in line behind the people who thought I should put plant poison on my lawn and the ones who didn't like my driving and...well, the list goes on.

When it appeared to be in the correct position, I disconnected the 911 operator, turned to go back to the front of the house and ran smack into a solid body.

Strong arms grabbed my shoulders. I went straight from panic mode to sheer terror mode. Had the mysterious man in black with a big gun and a big knife returned? I lifted my skillet to defend myself but recognized Fred before I delivered a fatal blow.

I lowered my skillet and he stepped back. "I was going to take care of that." He nodded toward the battered gas valve and took one of those multi-purpose tools that men carry from his pocket. "But it looks like your method, while a bit crude, worked."

I lifted a hand to my throat and tried to appear calm. "Is Sophie okay?"

"She's fine." He pointed to the far side of the street where Sophie stood in her white nightgown, arms wrapped around herself, obviously terrified. "Where's Rickie?"

"I sent him home even though that means I may not have a home when I get back over there."

"I wouldn't worry too much. He'll probably be sitting on the sofa with the television blaring, drinking a Coke."

"I guess he kind of saved Sophie's life tonight."

"Yes, but only because he was somewhere he shouldn't be."

Sirens sounded in the distance. Pleasant Grove's a small town. They didn't have far to travel.

"He'll get to tell his story to the cops," I said, heading to the front of the house to meet the EMTs and cops. "He'll get to be the center of attention."

The sirens got closer.

Fred sighed. "His fifteen minutes of fame are rapidly approaching."

I nodded. "I suppose he's entitled. Sort of."

"If you want to let him off the hook for the ring, I can slip it back into Sophie's house and nobody will ever know the difference."

"No way! He needs to learn that actions have consequences."

A fire truck and a police car pulled up. The doors flew open and firemen and cops piled out.

I looked at Fred and heaved a deep sigh. "I guess I'd better go get him so he can tell them his story. But as soon as they leave—"

"He has to face the consequences of stealing. Agreed."

As I crossed the street to my house, I noticed several neighbors opening windows and doors. We were going to have a middle of the night block party. Maybe I should pass out cookies.

I called Paula from my cell phone to tell her what was going on and to suggest she stay inside. She was happy to comply with that request.

As soon as I stepped onto my front porch, I knew Fred was right again. I could hear the TV even with the door closed. I went in and found Rickie sitting on the sofa, drinking a Coke.

"Come on," I said. "You get to tell your story and be a hero."

He sat forward excitedly. With enough Cokes, anybody would be excited. "Am I gonna be on television?"

I doubted that a gas leak in Pleasant Grove was going to make the morning news, but if I killed Rickie in front of the cops, that probably would. "Maybe," I said. "Come on."

Rickie grabbed his Coke and headed out the door. Perhaps he'd be on television and we'd get a free lifetime supply of Cokes for product placement.

By the time we got back to Sophie's house, the doors and windows were open and Fred and Sophie stood in the yard, talking to the cops. I didn't know either of the officers, and I wasn't going to call Trent in the middle of the night. He was homicide and so far no homicide had been committed.

Rickie got to be the star of the show. After about the third time he told his story, it became a little more coherent. I wasn't sure if that was because he was calming down and remembering or because he had more time to polish the story and make it believable. He continued to insist that the intruder had carried a gun and a knife and had threatened him with both. I questioned that last part, but it didn't matter. The essential part was true. Somebody had loosened the fittings on Sophie's new gas stove. If Rickie hadn't told someone, she would have died from inhaling the gas or it would have caught fire from the pilot light and her house would have exploded.

Just like her parents died.

భా

Finally all the uniforms left and the neighbors went back inside. Only Fred, Sophie, Rickie and I were left.

"They're not totally convinced a crime occurred," Fred said. "No evidence of a break in. No prints."

Rickie looked indignant. "I saw him!"

"I believe you. He must have worn gloves when he unscrewed the fitting. There is evidence somebody used a wrench. That's probably what you saw, Rickie, not a gun or knife."

"I saw a gun and a knife," Rickie said. "He would have killed me if I hadn't run away."

Sophie, wrapped in one of Fred's robes, stepped over to Rickie and hugged him, then leaned back and smiled. "Thank you for saving my life and my house."

Rickie grinned proudly.

I poked him in the ribs. "Tell her what you were doing at her house in the middle of the night."

He flinched but didn't back down. "I snuck out of Aunt Lindsay's house. I shouldn't have done that, but I'm awful glad you didn't die."

Fred held out the ring. "I think this is yours."

Sophie gasped, took the ring and slid it onto her finger. "It was my mother's. Where did you find it?"

Crickets chirped. A dog barked in the distance. Sophie looked from Fred to me and back to Fred, waiting for someone to answer.

I gave Rickie another nudge.

He looked down at the street. "I found it," he mumbled.

Sophie took Rickie's grubby little face between her hands, leaned over and kissed his grubby little forehead. "I left it on the kitchen table. That man must have taken it. You have definitely been my hero tonight."

I gritted my teeth and looked at Fred. He gave a slight shake of his head.

I didn't feel right letting Sophie think Rickie found her ring rather than stole it, but I would give Fred the chance to deal with the boy later. He seemed to know the secret to controlling him.

135

Fred draped an arm around Sophie's shoulders. "Let's go inside and get an overnight bag so you can spend the night in my guest room."

She nodded. "Thank you. If I walk in my sleep again, I won't have far to go." She smiled weakly. "And I won't risk leaving the door unlocked so somebody can come inside."

I grabbed Rickie's ear, a technique I'd learned from Rick's mother, and hauled him across the street.

I had about a half hour before it would be time to get up and go to work, and I intended to use that half hour to sleep if I had to bind and gag the kid.

ॐ∽ॐ

Paula's babysitter refused to take Rickie. She already had four children under her care and claimed that was the legal limit. My personal opinion was that she took one look at Rickie and made that up, but I didn't argue. I took him to the shop, set him down at the desk in the small room we used as an office and booted up the old laptop we kept there for Zach to play games on when he had to stay there.

"If you sit here and don't cause any problems, you can have unlimited Cokes and cookies. If you cause even the slightest problem, Fred's going to come get you." I picked up the new laptop we used for business and took it into the kitchen with me.

Paula looked up from rolling out biscuit dough. "I don't suppose you've had any word from Rick."

I set the laptop on top of the refrigerator where Rickie couldn't reach it just in case he tried. "No. I've left three messages, but I don't even know if he's getting them. If he is, I don't suppose he has any reason to call me. He wanted me to take care of Rickie in the first place, so he got his way."

"You think he really left the boy at his place all alone?"

"It's possible. It's also possible he gave him cab fare and told him to go to my house." I took down a bowl and began preparing my trademark chocolate chip cookies. "You seemed to get along well with Matthew at the barbecue." If she gave me her usual response, that she was just being polite, didn't want to get involved with anyone, blah, blah, blah, I wouldn't have to worry that he might be a psycho who drove around our neighborhood in the middle of the night in a white car.

She didn't look up from her work, but a tiny smile appeared on her lips. That was bad.

"He's nice," she said. "Zach likes him. He's coming over Saturday to take us out for pizza."

I swallowed around a big lump growing in my throat. "You're seeing him again on Saturday? That's a big step for somebody determined to live her life as a retroactive virgin."

She laughed softly. "For once, you may be right. Perhaps it's time for me to put the past behind me and trust someone again. I didn't trust you when I first met you, but now you're my best friend and I'd trust you with my life. Well, other than in an automobile."

Great. She trusted me and I might have introduced her to a nut job. Introduced her then convinced her to give him a chance to worm his way into her life and possibly break her heart. On the other hand, the only real evidence I had against him was based on Rickie's word which was about as reliable as his father's. If I told her my suspicions and she freaked out then I found that Rickie was lying and Matthew was a perfectly nice man, that would not be good. If I didn't tell her and Matthew turned out to be a stalker, that would not be good either. I had to find out about Matthew one way or the other soon.

I added a few extra chocolate chips to my cookies. Okay, I added a lot of extra chips. I had a feeling I was going to need them.

I didn't answer the first time Trent called my cell phone. We were in the middle of the breakfast rush. I figured the reason he was calling had something to do with the night before, that word got around that his girlfriend had called 911 and he wanted all the details. Well, he'd just have to wait while I dispensed chocolate.

When he called a second time fifteen minutes later, I started to get concerned. He knew my schedule and wouldn't normally call during that time.

As soon as I got a chance, I went into the kitchen to return his calls. But just as I took out my phone, it rang again. Fred. He never called during that time period either. I could only assume it must be important.

"Hello?"

"I know you're busy, so I'll keep this short. Sophie's going to keep your ex-husband's son this afternoon while you and I go out to Summerdale

Retirement Village to talk to the Murrays. She actually likes the kid." He hung up.

Brilliant! Cathy and Harold Murray had owned my house before I did. They would remember who, if anybody, had lived next door when Sophie and her parents were there. Not only would we get the answer to Carolyn's existence, I'd have an evening visiting with two people I really liked, and somebody else would have to deal with Rickie. Though I'd have to search him when I got home to make sure he didn't walk off with anything else that belonged to Sophie like a lamp or chair or coffee table.

The thief in question chose that moment to come out of the office. "I need another Coke." I took his glass and headed for the front.

The restaurant phone rang. Paula answered it and turned to me as I emerged from the kitchen. "It's Trent."

When he called on the business phone, that was a sign of disaster. Surely he couldn't be all that upset about my hobnobbing with the cops in the middle of the night. Something else must be going on.

I lifted the receiver to my ear. "I was just getting ready to—"

"Lindsay Powell?" The voice came from behind me. I turned to see two uniformed cops standing on the other side of the counter, looking grim.

"Hang on," I said to Trent and moved the phone receiver to my neck. "I'm Lindsay Powell. Can I help you?"

"We're here for the minor child Rickie Ganyon."

Chapter Thirteen

I gulped. Had they found out about the ring? Or something worse? What had he done now? "Okay," I squeaked.

"Is he here?" the cop asked.

"Can you hold on just a minute?" I put the phone back to my ear. "What's going on?" I asked Trent. "Why are the cops looking for Rickie?"

"There's an Amber Alert out for him," he said.

"What? Who reported him? Is Rick back in town? His mother?"

"Turns out Rick didn't leave him alone in his house. He left him with neighbors. When they got up Saturday morning and found him gone, they immediately reported him missing. As soon as I got in this morning and heard about it, I told them you had the boy. I've been trying to get hold of you to tell you to bring him in."

"Ma'am," the cop said, rudely interrupting my conversation with Trent, "is the minor child Rickie Ganyon on these premises?"

"Yes."

"Would you take us to him?"

"Yes, I can do that. Trent, I have to go now." I hung up the phone and looked around the room. There were only a few customers left in the restaurant, but we certainly had everybody's attention. I usually like attention but not that kind.

I led the rude cops to the back.

Rickie looked up from his video game when we entered the office. His big eyes got even bigger at the sight of the uniforms. He stood, his gaze darting around the room as if searching for a way out or a place to hide. It was a small room, and the only way out was the door where the two cops and I stood.

"Are you Rickie Ganyon?"

He lifted his small, pointed chin and stared back fiercely. "Who wants to know?" I had to give him credit for guts.

The officer knelt in front of him, getting down to his level, and smiled. "The Fergusons have been worried about you, Rickie. They'd like for you to return to their house."

Rickie backed away. "I won't!"

The officer frowned. "Why not?"

"I don't like them people! They—" He hesitated, looking directly and intently into the man's eyes. I knew that look and that hesitation. I'd seen his father do it often enough. He was taking time to make up a lie. "They were mean to me."

"What did they do to you that was mean? Did they hurt you?"

Rickie held out his thin arms which were covered in scratches and puckered up his face as if he was about to cry. "They did this to me."

"Oh, stop it," I snapped. "You got those scratches last night when you were climbing around in that tree!"

"Is that true, Rickie? Did you get those scratches last night instead of from the Fergusons?"

"I'm not going back! They don't like me. They beat me and they don't feed me."

The officer rose. "Why don't we all go down to the station and sort this out?"

Rickie folded his arms obdurately. "No."

I folded my arms the same way. "You'll have to get out the cuffs, officer."

Rickie looked interested. "You got handcuffs?"

"I've got handcuffs and a radio in the car and—"

"And Cokes," I said. "He'll give you a Coke if you go to the station with him."

Rickie shrugged and let the officer guide him out the door. "Am I being arrested?"

"No," the cop said.

"Yes," I said.

Rickie looked kind of pleased at that prospect.

I watched him heading toward the door with the officer. Did I feel a tiny bit of regret that our visit was over? To be completely honest, I felt an enormous sense of relief. I suppose it's one thing if you give birth to a child and have him around from the beginning, but having a nine year old demon child suddenly thrust on me was more of a challenge than I wanted.

"You too, ma'am," the second cop said, effectively ending my good feelings.

"Me?" I pointed to myself. "You want me to go to the station with you?"

"Yes, ma'am."

I really wished they'd quit with the *ma'am* business. Made me feel ninety years old. "Why do you need me to come with you? I trust you with the kid."

"You were in possession of a minor child who disappeared under unknown circumstances. We need you to come down and make a statement."

"*Unknown circumstances?* Surely you don't think I kidnapped him! Nobody in their right mind would kidnap that boy! He came to my house and told me his father left him alone and he had nowhere to go! Ask him! He'll tell you." Actually I had no idea what Rickie would tell them.

"Why didn't you call social services?"

"Because social services sucks."

"Yes, ma'am."

This wasn't going very well. I really didn't want to be hauled in on kidnapping charges. "Look, it's not like the boy's a stranger. He's my ex-husband's son."

"Yes, ma'am."

I swallowed hard. "Are you going to arrest me for taking the kid in?"

"We just need you to come down and make a statement."

I could feel the steel bars closing around me. Who'd take care of Henry? How would Trent feel having a jailbird for a girlfriend? "He's my stepson, for crying out loud!"

Oh, God! Had I really said that? Some words should never be uttered even in the interest of staying out of jail. I shouldn't be talking without a lawyer. I was glad no one else was around to hear that insane statement.

"Yes, ma'am."

I sighed. "Let me get my purse. Can we go out the back door so the customers won't think I'm being arrested?"

"No, ma'am. Our car's parked out front."

Great. I had to do a perp walk through my own restaurant. Maybe I could serve Perp Walk Brownies tomorrow. There's nothing like a good crime to make people hungry and rev up sales.

తొళ

I got out of jail. Trent vouched for me, swore I made every effort to find out where Rickie belonged and that the kid really did tell me he'd been abandoned at his father's house. They released me with my record if not my dignity intact in time to get back and help Paula clean up after closing.

I had no idea what Rickie told them, and I really didn't care. I was just relieved he was no longer my problem. My world could get back to normal. Make chocolate, serve chocolate, eat chocolate, feed Henry.

As soon as I got home and fed Henry, Fred and I took his vintage Mercedes across town to Summerdale Retirement Village where Cathy and Harold Murray, the former owners of my house, lived.

Since first meeting the older couple a year ago we'd stayed in touch and become friends. They popped into Death by Chocolate regularly, but we didn't get to spend a lot of time together because the Murrays kept a busy schedule...dances, dinners, card games, board games, movies, golf, bicycling and walking. They were fun people. I looked forward to seeing them again.

Cathy greeted us at the door with a wide smile. "Come in. Oh, you brought more of those wonderful cookies!"

Harold came up behind his wife, hair the same shade of white as hers, blue eyes twinkling behind thick glasses. "Come in, come in. Cathy even cleaned house because you were coming."

Cathy punched him playfully. "Stop that!"

We entered the sunny, cheerful apartment that reflected the personality of its inhabitants.

"I'll be right back with something to drink," Cathy said, heading toward the kitchen.

Fred and I sat on the muted mauve sofa and Harold sank into a chair.

"Have you been playing golf in this heat?" I asked.

"I get up early every morning before it gets hot."

"I've seen him play when the temperature was over a hundred," Cathy called from the kitchen. "He's obsessed."

Harold grinned. "It's true. I'm making up for all those years when I had to spend my days in an office instead of on a golf course."

Cathy returned with a large tray holding three cups of coffee, one Coke and a plate heaped with the cookies I'd brought.

"Now," she said, setting the tray on the coffee table and taking a seat in the other chair, "tell me what's been going on. Are you still dating that nice policeman?"

"I am, and now that Rick's almost out of the picture, we're having a lot more fun."

Cathy's forehead beneath her white curls wrinkled with a frown. "*Almost*? Your divorce was final, wasn't it?"

I sighed, took a long drink of my Coke and launched into an abbreviated story of how I had come to babysit my ex-husband's son for two days. Fred sipped his coffee and waited patiently while I finished with the trivia. Actually, while he appeared to be waiting patiently, I could feel the tension vibrating from him. He's not big on chit-chat.

"If that ever happens again, you just bring the boy over here and let Harold and me babysit," Cathy offered.

"I would never do that to you. Rickie is a demon child." Of course, I was talking to the couple who continued to believe their grandson George would one day come home from prison, go to college and become a model citizen.

Cathy gave a tinkling laugh. "All kids seem like that from time to time. They just need love and guidance."

I couldn't deny that Rickie had received very little of either of those things. Would he have been a different child if he'd been raised by someone like the Murrays?

We talked about the dances and dinners the Murrays had gone to, how much they'd won the last time they went to the casino, new desserts I'd created at Death by Chocolate, and how Paula and Zach were doing. I didn't tell them about the possibility of Paula having a man in her life. The Murrays would love to hear that. They wanted everybody to be as happy as they were. But Paula's love life could wait until I was certain how it was going to turn out.

At a lull in the conversation Cathy folded her hands in her lap and exchanged a smile with her husband. "We have some exciting news."

My lips automatically moved upward to form a smile, expecting to hear they were going on a cruise or buying a new car or getting a dog.

"George just had a parole hearing, and it looks like he may get to come home."

George, their drug-dealing grandson whose activities had almost got me killed a year ago. My smile froze in place.

"The new attorney we hired," Harold said. "Guy's really good. He got some evidence overturned and showed the parole board that George is trying to turn his life around."

"When he gets home, he's going to get his GED and go to college."

"That's great," I said. "Does he have any idea what he wants to be?" Though he was pre-qualified to be a pharmacist, he'd probably have a little trouble getting licensed in that field.

Cathy shrugged and reached for another cookie. "He'll figure it out after he takes a few classes."

"We know it won't be easy," Harold said, "but we'll do all we can to help him. George has had some problems, but the boy has a good heart."

I thought of the angry man Fred and I had visited in prison, of the darkness that lived in the back of his eyes. But he had sounded sincere when he said he loved his grandparents. Anything was possible. If the Murrays were able to rehabilitate George, maybe even Rickie could become an upstanding citizen.

"When he comes home, we're going to have a party for him, and we'd love for you all to come."

It took a couple of heartbeats for me to catch my breath and respond. "Of course we'll be there."

Fred was silent. I elbowed him.

"Yes," he said. "We'll be there."

"I'll bake a chocolate cake for him," I promised. That would be the easy part of that event.

Cathy beamed. Harold smiled. I got the feeling he wasn't quite as certain as his wife that George was going to become the perfect grandson.

Then we got to the subject of our new neighbor.

"Do you remember Sophie Fleming?" Fred asked. "She lived across the street about twenty-five years ago."

Cathy poured more coffee for Fred. She must make really good coffee for him to go beyond the polite first cup. "Of course we remember the Flemings," she said. "Sophie was the cutest little thing with those big brown eyes and all that dark, shiny hair. She was a live wire. Never met a stranger. We babysat her a couple of times, but the Flemings didn't go out often. They were young and struggling. What happened to them after they moved to Nebraska was so sad."

Cathy's description of Sophie as a bubbly little girl presented a contrast with the adult Sophie. Of course we all grow up and change, but I suspected Sophie's early losses had a lot to do with her change.

"Did you know the family was planning to move?" I asked.

Cathy shook her head. "No, it was all very strange. He had a decent job, possibility of moving up in the company. They loved the house and had some kind of arrangement where they could buy it for no down payment if they did enough improvements. They seemed perfectly happy and settled one day. Then the next, they were gone."

"That was the year we had all the big floods in Missouri," Harold said. "It rained almost every day, so we didn't get outside as much as usual, but still, we'd see them in their yard in between showers, go over and talk. Everything seemed fine. Then one morning when I was leaving for work, I saw the moving van pull up to their door."

"I went over to talk to them," Cathy said. "They seemed different. They were usually friendly and relaxed. Very nice people. But that day they seemed tense. When I asked why they were moving, Bob said he got an offer he couldn't turn down. Jan didn't say anything. In fact, she barely looked at me. She just kept packing. I asked what kind of job it was, and he wouldn't say."

"How did Sophie handle the move?" Fred asked.

Cathy shook her head. "I don't know. She wouldn't come out of her room. I assumed she was devastated because she'd have to leave her home and her friend. You know how attached kids become at that age. I wanted to go in and talk to her, but they wouldn't let me."

Fred and I exchanged glances and both sat forward. "Her friend?" I repeated. "She had to leave her friend?"

"Yes, the little girl who lived in your house, Fred. Little blonde-haired beauty. I think her name was Carolyn."

Chapter Fourteen

Carolyn was real, not imaginary. She had lived and died in Fred's house, and Sophie had seen her friend murdered.

I looked at Fred. He looked at me.

Thick silence filled the small room, broken only by the raspy song of cicadas calling from the trees outside and the ticking of the Murrays' grandfather clock over in the corner.

I didn't realize how long we'd been quiet, assimilating what it all meant, until Cathy spoke again. "Did I say something wrong?"

"No, of course not," I assured her. "It's just that, well, Sophie thinks Carolyn was only her imaginary friend, that she didn't really exist."

Cathy set her cup on the coffee table and looked up. She wasn't smiling anymore. "That poor girl. Losing her best friend and then her parents, I suppose it's only natural that her life before that would seem like a dream. Maybe that's the only way she could deal with everything that happened."

Harold sat forward in his chair, reached over and took his wife's hand. "That's sad, not to remember a friend. She doesn't think her parents were imaginary too, does she?"

I bit my lip. I didn't want to tell them the Flemings, people they'd liked, had lied to their daughter. That was something they probably didn't want to hear.

"No, she remembers her parents." Fred had no such emotional compunctions. "It's just Carolyn. The reason she thinks the girl is imaginary is because that's what her parents told her."

Harold frowned. "That's strange. Why would they do that?"

A very good question, one to which I had no answer.

"But you met Carolyn?" Fred moved closer to the edge of the sofa and set his cup on the table beside Cathy's. He was as intent as I'd ever seen him. Still about two on a scale of one to ten, but for Fred, that was pretty intent. "You actually saw her?"

Cathy looked at me questioningly as if she didn't understand why Fred would need verification of what she'd already told him. I shrugged. I wasn't responsible for Fred's eccentricities.

"Yes," she said. "We saw her. Lots of times. She was a quiet little blonde girl. Sophie's opposite in all ways, but the two were best friends. She was very real. Not imaginary, I assure you."

"How about her parents? Did you know them?" Fred leaned forward, hands on his knees. Extremely intent, relatively speaking.

Cathy and Harold exchanged glances and Harold made a noise that almost sounded like a snort. "They were a little unusual."

Coming from the people who contended their drug dealer grandson was *a good boy*, that could only mean Carolyn's parents had been *very* unusual.

"Carolyn's mother stayed pretty close to home," Cathy said. "I tried to talk to her several times, but she never had much to say. She was kind of shy but seemed like a really nice person, a good mother. But the father—" She looked at Harold.

Cathy wasn't the type woman who looked to her husband for permission to say something. I waited for them to tell me the father had horns and a tail.

Harold shook his head and compressed his lips. Off the top of my head I'd say they really disliked Carolyn's father. "He wasn't there a lot."

"She said he traveled." Cathy arched an eyebrow as if to say she did not for one minute believe the man travelled.

"He visited a couple of times a week." Harold lifted his hands, palms up. "I admit, when he was there, everything seemed to be fine. He took them places, played with Carolyn. From what we saw, Sarah and Carolyn both adored him."

"Her name was Sarah?" I asked. We had a name for Carolyn's mother. That made her real too. But where was she? Murdered along with Carolyn? Or was she the murderer?

"Yes," Cathy affirmed. "Her first name was Sarah." She hesitated and again looked at her husband.

"She never gave us her last name," Harold said. "We don't think she was married to Carolyn's father. We do think he was married to somebody, just not her."

Cathy nodded in agreement.

Now we were getting somewhere. Dr. Dan Jamison had owned the house, and he was married to somebody, somebody with enough money to keep him in medical school and take care of his younger

153

brother, somebody he wouldn't want to discover he had a mistress on the side. Would he kill his mistress and his daughter to keep that wife with all the money?

"Do you know the father's name?" Fred asked.

I gulped the last of my Coke and set the can on the table, all my attention focused on the Murrays.

Harold looked at his wife. "Do you remember his name? Sarah always referred to him as her husband, and Carolyn called him *Daddy*. But one day when I saw them in the yard, I strolled over to introduce myself. Made him look me in the eye and shake my hand even though it was pretty obvious he didn't want to." Harold frowned. "Now what the heck was his name? Something simple. Ben? Jim? Tom? Dave?"

"Dan?" I suggested. Okay, I was putting words in his mouth, but it wasn't like we were on a quiz show and he was required to figure out the answer all by himself.

Harold snapped his fingers. "Dan! That's it. But he wouldn't give me a last name."

"This Dan, what did he look like?" Fred asked.

"He was quite good looking," Cathy said. "Tall, brown hair, brown eyes."

Dr. Dan, the Plastics Man.

"What did Sarah look like?" I asked.

"Blond hair, blue eyes, fair skin, just like Carolyn. She was a pretty little thing."

"Did she work?"

"No. She was proud to be a stay-at-home mom."

I thought of the picture in Dr. Dan's office. His wife was blond, but my mother's description of Natalie Jamison did not fit with the image of Carolyn's mom. *Shy, proud to be a stay-at-home mom?* Besides, Natalie would never live in an old house in my neighborhood. No, definitely not the same blonde.

"When did they move away?" Fred asked.

"It's hard to say exactly when since we didn't see them very often, but it was the same year the Flemings moved, the year we had all the flooding."

"Did you see them move out?" I asked. "Did a van show up one day like with the Flemings?"

Cathy shook her head. "No. They just disappeared. One day we saw a *For Sale* sign in the yard. We thought maybe the father finally did the right thing, married her and maybe moved to another town. Why are you asking all these questions? Has something happened to Sarah and Carolyn?"

Fred leaned back in a semblance of his usual casual demeanor. "We're not sure. We'd just like to find them. You never heard from them after they moved? A letter, a phone call?"

"No. Not a word. I often wondered what happened to them, but about that time we started having problems with George, so we really weren't paying a lot of attention to anything outside our own family." She looked from one of us to the other, concern obvious on her face. "What's going on?"

I didn't see any reason to keep the truth from her. They weren't suspects and we weren't pretending to be somebody like mold experts or stripper talent scouts. "Maybe nothing," I said. "Or maybe something. Sophie keeps having a nightmare about Carolyn being dead."

Cathy lifted her hands to the sides of her face. "Oh no!" She looked at Harold then back at us. "But it's only a dream, right, a bad dream because living in that house has brought up memories of her childhood friend?" I could tell when she asked the question that she knew that wasn't what I meant but Cathy and Harold are the ultimate optimists.

"No, we think she actually saw Carolyn die. When she was five years old. In Fred's house."

Cathy sucked in a sharp breath. "Did *he* kill her?"

I didn't have to ask who *he* was. The father. Dr. Dan. "We don't know. Maybe."

"Did he kill Sarah too?" Cathy's pleasant features were horror-stricken.

"Maybe," I said.

"Lindsay, you're speculating," Fred protested. "We don't know for sure that anybody was killed. All we have is Sophie's dream."

"Memory," I corrected. "We have her description of that poor little girl being murdered and we have the fact that Sarah and Carolyn disappeared the same time Sophie's family moved away followed by the death of her parents under mysterious circumstances."

Cathy's eyes widened. "I didn't know the Flemings died under mysterious circumstances."

"They died from a gas leak, and last night somebody tried to kill Sophie by creating a gas leak in her house."

I had everybody's attention, but not in a good way. The Murrays were upset and Fred was annoyed. For the second time that day I realized that attention is not always a good thing.

☞☜

It was getting dark by the time we left the Murrays with promises to let them know what we discovered about Carolyn and her mother, to have them over one evening so they could meet Sophie and to attend a party at their place when George came home.

"Why didn't you want me to tell them what we suspect?" I asked as Fred drove toward home, never exceeding the speed limit, poking along as if we had all the time in the world.

"Because we don't know for sure that Carolyn's dead."

"How sure do you need to be?"

"A body would be adequate proof."

"Fine. We'll rip up the floorboards in your bedroom and see if we can find a body."

He ignored me and turned a corner, keeping all four wheels on the ground. I'd driven that car once, and it had a lot of wasted power.

"Hey!" I turned toward him. "That's not a bad idea!"

"Rip up my floorboards? It's a terrible idea!"

"Not rip up your floorboards. I mean the other idea that occurred to me after I said that. We should get some luminol and test your floor and walls for blood."

"Actually, that's not a bad idea except I had the floors sanded and resurfaced and new sheetrock on the walls before I moved in."

"Damn! Why do you have to be so fastidious? I don't suppose—"

His gaze left the road long enough to shoot me a glare. "No, I did not save the old sheetrock or the sawdust."

I folded my arms. "You picked a lousy time to ignore your OCD tendencies."

"Do you want to go to Sophie's with me to tell her what we learned tonight?"

I looked at him smugly. "So you admit we did learn something?"

"We learned that Daniel Jamison may be Carolyn's father. We don't even know that for sure, but perhaps we can use that information to spark Sophie's memories. Maybe she'll remember seeing him when we describe him."

He just couldn't admit he was wrong.

Fred pulled his car into the garage and we got out and started across the street. We were halfway there when Sophie's porch light came on and her front door opened.

Interesting. "Think she has dinner waiting for us?" I suddenly realized I was hungry. Chocolate chip cookies are great, but they only go so far. I was ready for a pizza, double pepperoni, extra cheese.

Fred took my elbow and urged me forward at a faster pace. "Something's wrong."

Since I knew Fred could see her expression with his telescopic night vision, I hurried.

"Come in," she said when we stepped onto the porch. I could hear the tension in her voice and see it on her face. Once again, Fred was right. "There's something you need to see."

Chapter Fifteen

We followed her inside and I stared in awe at the beautiful living area she'd created from the ugliness that had been there before. High ceiling, hardwood floors, a plush off-white sofa with colorful pillows and inviting chairs in matching colors, wall decorations and pictures that looked as if they had been fashioned just for that room. It was a room created by an interior designer. It was Sophie.

Except for the rectangular cardboard box sitting on the coffee table and its ghastly contents.

Sophie took a seat on the end of the sofa, as far away from the box as she could get, and folded her hands in her lap. "That was waiting on my porch when I got home from work."

Fred sat down directly in front of the box and leaned closer. "Have you touched it?"

"I touched the box but not the doll."

The baby doll was old, at least twenty years. It looked like something I'd played with when I was young. In fact, it looked very much like some of my dolls. Her blond hair was matted, her dress was dirty, and her head had been severed from her body. Not that I decapitated my dolls deliberately. It just happened. But this one did not look like an accident.

The incision appeared to be recent and precise, as if done with a sharp surgeon's knife.

"That's Carolyn's doll," Sophie said quietly. "She was real."

"Yes," Fred agreed. "She was real. Are you certain this was her doll?"

She nodded. "When I opened the box, the memory of the day she got that doll hit me hard. It was a birthday gift from her father."

I sank into a turquoise chair, and *sank into* was the right phrase. It was soft and plush and molded to my body. I could sit there for a day or two if somebody would bring me chocolate and pizza. "You remember her father?" I asked.

She bit her lip and nodded. "Yes. I don't think he lived with them. Maybe they were divorced. But when he came to visit, Carolyn was ecstatic. He always brought her toys, and usually he'd bring something for me too."

That picture didn't exactly coincide with the impression I had of Dr. Dan. But people thought Ted Bundy was a nice man.

Fred took Sophie's arm gently. He'd never taken my arm gently.

But he had fetched me a Coke with a straw when I was in the hospital after being poisoned. Okay, I had seen Fred's gentle side before. Still, the way he was looking at Sophie was…gentle.

"Sophie," he said quietly, "I need you to do something that's not going to be easy."

She nodded, her dark gaze focused trustingly on his face. Of course I trust Fred…with my life. But not with that total, unquestioning trust I saw in her eyes. I was going to have to talk to Sophie about the mistake of giving that complete trust to anybody, even Fred.

"I want you to lean back, relax, close your eyes and focus on that scene you keep dreaming about, Carolyn's death. I want you to tell me every detail you see, what she's wearing, what the room looks like, any other people you can see."

Obediently she leaned back against an emerald green pillow. Instead of making her look like a corpse, the color brightened her skin. If I didn't like her, I could hate her.

Fred held her hand in one of his and stroked it with the other. That was a little much. I made a face and tried to get his attention, but he was focused completely on Sophie.

"Relax, Sophie. Let the clouds swirl around you and take you to a safe place. The clouds are warm and comfortable. They're settling around you, wrapping you in their warmth. You're going to remember your dream about Carolyn, but it's going to be like watching a movie, not like you're really there."

Omigawd! He was hypnotizing her! I knew she shouldn't trust him so completely!

I sat forward and started to protest, to break the spell. But I couldn't think of any reason why I should, so I kept my mouth shut and watched in fascination. Fred continued to speak softly to Sophie. I made a note to stay wide awake if he ever spoke softly to me.

"Sophie, can you see Carolyn?"

"Yes."

"What's she doing?"

She rolled her head and gave a slight moan.

"Relax. You're watching a movie. You're not personally involved. Where are you while you're watching this movie, Sophie?"

"Hiding in the bedroom closet." Her voice was small, like that of a child. That was creepy.

"Why are you hiding in the bedroom closet?"

"I wasn't sleepy so I sneaked out and came over to play with Carolyn. I'm not supposed to go outside at night."

"So you came over to see Carolyn in the middle of the night. Why are you hiding in the closet?"

"Somebody came to see her mommy. We heard them yelling, and then we heard somebody coming upstairs, so I hid in the closet. I didn't want her mommy to tell my mommy. I'd get in trouble."

"Who came to see Carolyn's mommy?"

Sophie fidgeted. "He hurt Carolyn."

"Relax." He stroked her hand again until she calmed and her breathing was once more quiet and even. "Did this person come into Carolyn's room?"

"Yes."

"What happened when he came into her room?"

"She cried. He hurt her. He had a knife. I was scared. I got out of the closet and ran home and told Mommy and Daddy."

"Did you see the person who hurt Carolyn?"

She shook her head slowly from side to side. "I didn't want to look. Carolyn was bleeding."

"Did you see the face of the person who hurt her?"

"No, but Mommy and Daddy saw him."

I sat forward. That got my attention.

Fred showed no sign that he was surprised, but I knew he was. Well, I thought maybe he was.

"When did your mommy and daddy see him?"

"He tried to get me and hurt me too. He chased me home. Mommy sent me to my room and they talked to him for a long time."

"What did they say?"

"I don't know. I was in my room crying because Carolyn got hurt. When he left, Mommy came up to my room. She was crying too."

"What did your mommy say when she came to your room?"

"She hugged me and said I should go to sleep and everything would be okay when I woke up."

"I want you to focus on that moment you ran out of the closet and went past the man who hurt Carolyn. You caught a glimpse of him. Focus on that glance. Isolate it from the rest of the movie and look at that one frame."

She moved her head from side to side and gave a small whimper. I think Fred flinched when she made that sound. Maybe he just burped. Hard to tell in the dim light.

"Can you see the man who hurt Carolyn?"

"Sort of."

"Was that man her father?"

Sophie was quiet for a long time. "Maybe," she finally said.

"Was he tall?"

"Yes."

"Was his hair dark or light?"

"Dark, like mine."

"Can you tell me anything else about him?"

She clenched her hands into fists. "He hurt Carolyn."

Fred looked at me as if asking if I had any comments or questions. I shrugged and let out a long breath I suddenly realized I'd been holding, unable to breathe while Sophie told her story.

"Sophie, when I tell you to open your eyes, you're going to be wide awake. You'll feel rested and refreshed. You'll remember everything you've seen, but it will be like a movie. You won't be upset. Open your eyes, Sophie."

She did, lifted her hands to her face and promptly burst into tears.

Apparently he wasn't as good at the hypnosis thing as he thought he was.

He looked at me and for the first time I saw panic on his face.

I sat upright, held my arms out in a semblance of an embrace, and mouthed the words, "Hug her!"

He wrapped tentative arms around Sophie. "Relax," he said. "It's only a movie."

I dashed to the kitchen and was relieved to see that Sophie had Cokes in her refrigerator. I grabbed one and took it to her.

When I returned, she'd regained her composure for the most part and was wiping her eyes with a tissue. "Thank you," she said as she accepted the Coke. "I'm sorry. I didn't mean to break down like that. It's just that now that I know Carolyn was real, her death hit me like it happened yesterday." She smiled at Fred. "It's not your fault. I cry at sad movies."

Fred sat beside her, once again in control, but now I had his number. He could take down a murderer with a well-aimed kick, drink coffee with mobsters with no worries and hack into government files without a second thought, but he didn't know what to do with a crying woman.

"I'm sorry I brought up painful memories," he said.

She shook her head. "They were always there, tormenting me behind the scenes. They had to come out eventually. Now we need to find the man who murdered Carolyn."

"You're certain she was dead?"

"When I ran out of that room, she was lying on the floor, covered in blood, and that man was standing over her with a knife. I never saw her again. And now this doll—" She waved a hand at the box on her coffee table. "Yes, I'm certain she's dead."

"What about her mother? Did you see her that night?"

"No. She wasn't in Carolyn's room. Only the man came upstairs. Do you think he killed her too?"

"At this point, we don't know what happened to her. Can you tell me anything else about the man's face?"

She wadded the tissue in her hand. "I was so upset about Carolyn, I didn't pay any attention to him. I didn't look at his face. He appeared to be a monster, tall and dark, a monster who hurt my friend and wanted to hurt me. You think it might have been her father?"

"It's possible. You said earlier her father was a kind man. Do you remember anything else about him? Was he abusive? Did he spank Carolyn? Anything to suggest he could be a killer?"

She shook her head. "I don't remember him ever spanking Carolyn. The only times she got in trouble were when I instigated something, and then her mother would send me home and send her to her room."

"How did he act around Carolyn's mother?"

"They were affectionate, often hugging, holding hands. Once Carolyn and I caught them kissing, and we giggled about that for days. I can't imagine that he killed her. Maybe it was a home invasion."

"That's always possible. But if the killer followed you home, why didn't your parents call the police?"

She frowned. "I don't know. Maybe he threatened them."

Or bribed them. I thought of the large deposit made to the Flemings' bank account and their sudden move out of state.

Had their deaths been a tragic accident or the result of someone who didn't trust them to keep his secret?

"Please." She gazed intently into Fred's eyes. "Find out who killed my friend."

He gazed intently into her eyes. I felt sort of like an intruder. "I'll try my best," he promised.

I stood, ready to sneak out and leave them alone. But Fred rose too, and Sophie stood with him.

167

"I think you should plan to spend the night at my house again," he said.

She smiled bravely. "I'll be fine. My deadbolt is quite secure, and now that I've faced reality and brought up the memory, I don't think I'll have the Carolyn nightmare again. That means I won't be leaving my house with the door open."

He nodded. "If you do, I'll come over here with you and check the place thoroughly."

We left and she stood in the doorway watching us.

We reached the end of the sidewalk and stepped off the curb onto the street. "You ever been in love?" I asked.

"I suppose that depends on how you define the word," he replied. "Would you say you're in love with chocolate?"

Of course I wasn't going to get a straight answer out of him.

"Wait!" Sophie called.

We turned as she hurried down the porch steps toward us.

"I think I remember something else." She gave Fred an uncertain look then continued. "The man, just before Carolyn cried out, he said, *I'm sorry.*"

I looked at Fred and could tell he was thinking the same thing I was thinking. Did Dr. Dan suffer remorse because he was forced to kill his second family to maintain his first?

Chapter Sixteen

The next day while Paula and I prepared for breakfast, I caught her up on the latest developments. She listened quietly for the most part, shaking her head now and then, but when I finished the story about our visit to the Murrays, she stopped beating the cinnamon roll dough and looked at me in a way that made me feel she wanted to replace that dough with my head.

"You promised them you'd go to a party for George?"

"Well, yeah, actually I promised them you, Fred and I would go to that party."

Her eyes widened and she gave the dough a really hard thump. "I'd kill you right now, but then who'd make the Triple Chocolate Mousse Cake for lunch?"

It's always good to know my talents are appreciated.

The morning went smoothly. One customer demanded his money back after he'd eaten three chocolate scones and drunk two cups of Paula's coffee. But nobody died, the police didn't come to take me away, no reporters came by to ask embarrassing questions, so it was a good morning.

Matthew came in toward the end of the lunch hour rush, sat at the counter and talked to Paula at every opportunity. He had a goofy expression on his face when he looked at her. I was suddenly glad I hadn't shared my reservations about him. Obviously I was wrong. Anybody who looked like that couldn't possibly have an ulterior motive.

Finally only a few people remained, Matthew among them, of course. I was beginning cleanup when Fred called. I took my tray of dishes into the kitchen, set them in the sink and answered my cell phone.

"Do you have a long skirt?" As I said, Fred isn't a fan of chitchat.

"I think so."

"What color is it?"

"Red, purple, green, orange, teal. I dressed as a hippie for a Halloween party. It gets in my way when I walk, so I haven't worn it since."

"That won't do. You need a black one."

"Are we making a visit to the cult people?"

"How about a scarf?"

"I have several scarves."

"What color?"

"Red, purple, green, orange, teal. I like bright colors."

He sighed. "I'll take care of it. I've been doing some checking on our favorite doctor, and I've located his parents. He and his brother are both from Seventh Gate."

A cold hand wrapped around my heart and squeezed really tight. "So he and Matthew are from the same community." That didn't prove anything bad about Matthew, but it looked suspicious.

"I'll bring the necessary clothing to your house when you get home from work." He hung up.

I stood motionless, staring at my phone for several moments.

Paula shoved the door open and almost ran into me. "What are you doing?" she asked as she placed a tray of dirty dishes on the counter.

"Uh…"

"Is there any more Mousse Cake?" She opened the refrigerator door. "Oh, good, there's another one. Matthew wants a piece. I told him it's your best creation to date." She set the dessert on the counter and began to slice it. "He's worried about Zach and me after what happened to Sophie Sunday night. He offered to sit outside in his car all night to be sure we were safe. I told him that was silly."

She didn't look up, but I could tell from her voice that, while she thought Matthew's offer was silly, she also thought it was sweet. I thought he'd just set up a perfect alibi for hanging around and spying on Sophie.

I watched Paula carefully place a piece of Triple Chocolate Mousse Cake on a plate then take it out front. I considered taking the remainder of the dessert and dumping it over Matthew's head, but that would have been a waste of good chocolate.

Still, it was tempting.

☙❧

True to his word, Fred met me at the front door of my house when I got home from work. He wore a pair of faded overalls and a blue work shirt and carried a large shopping bag with no store name on it. I suspected he had not bought our new clothes at

Macy's. Maybe the back room of the Good Will thrift store.

I opened the door and Henry greeted me, winding himself around my legs and purring. He ignored Fred and Fred ignored him. Before we left, Henry would somehow manage to stick a couple hundred of his hairs to Fred's clothing.

I fed Henry while Fred unpacked his bag in the living room.

I returned to see a long black skirt, a black blouse and a black scarf spread out on the sofa. They were all faded and wrinkled. "Haute couture."

"Go upstairs and put them on. Wear those black shoes you wear when your feet hurt. We need to hurry. It's a long drive."

"If we're in a hurry, does this mean I get to drive since I drive faster than you?"

He scowled. "We'll see."

He didn't say no.

I gathered up the dreadful clothes and took them to my bedroom where I pulled off my jeans and T-shirt then put on the witch's disguise. I studied myself in the cheval floor mirror. I looked sort of like a witch. Was this how those people we were going to visit dressed? How sad to be forced to wear clothes like this all the time...no blue jeans, no red silk shirts, no fleecy warm-ups in winter.

If Dr. Dan grew up in an environment like that, no wonder he was a psycho killer.

I folded the scarf, tucked it under my arm and went back downstairs. Henry and Fred were both waiting at the front door. Fred's clothes were liberally sprinkled with white cat hairs.

I let one guy outside and asked for car keys from the other. Fred shook his head. "I don't think it's worth it. Even if you drive fifteen miles over the speed limit the entire way, we'll only get there six and a half minutes faster."

"It could be a critical six and a half minutes."

"I was rounding. It would really only be six minutes and twenty-one seconds." He grimaced, sighed and handed me the keys. "You'll hit some heavy traffic, so you'll have to go more than twenty miles over the limit on the highway to make up for lost time."

I smiled. "Not a problem."

We were walking across my yard to his car when a dark sedan pulled up in front of my house and stopped. The back passenger door flew open and a small figure that was becoming way too familiar tumbled out and ran toward me.

Rickie.

That wasn't possible. I was hallucinating. Somebody put something in that last Coke.

A man and woman stepped out of the car. John and Cara Ferguson. Rick's friends he'd entrusted with his son. I'd glimpsed them briefly at the police station when the cops had dragged me in for questioning.

"Aunt Lindsay! I'm home!" Rickie ran up and threw his skinny little arms around my waist. "I missed you so much."

"What's going on?" I tried to loosen Rickie's grip, but he held on like a demented tick.

173

John took the bulging canvas bag from the trunk of his car, and the couple approached slowly. They looked different than they'd looked at the police station, less like a preppy couple living the good life and more like parents. Cara's short blond hair was no longer perfect and her makeup was smeared. John's immaculate white shirt was streaked with something. Dirt? Chocolate? His eyes bulged slightly and he had a scratch on one cheek.

John set the familiar canvas bag down in front of me, and Cara smiled tightly. "You're Lindsay Powell?" she asked.

I looked at Fred, hoping he'd come up with a good story to get me out of the current situation.

"She is." He sold me out. "Who are you?"

"He'll be better off with you." John took his wife's arm and tugged her back toward their car.

"No!" I tried unsuccessfully to push Rickie away. "He's supposed to stay with you! I got in trouble for letting him stay with me. The cops tried to arrest me for kidnapping. It's illegal for him to stay with me!"

"But you told them you're his stepmother. It's okay for you to keep him." Cara turned to leave.

I tried to stumble after them but found it difficult to make progress with a nine-year old succubus attached to my body.

"Fred, help me!" I pleaded.

"You told them you're his stepmother?" Fred was visibly astonished. That doesn't happen often.

"I was desperate."

"Why would you do something like that?"

"You had to be there."

The Fergusons slid into their car, slammed the door and laid rubber as they drove away.

I gave up the attempt to catch them and merely watched their departing car in horror, my heart sinking to the bottom of my big toe. That was probably the fastest they'd ever driven in their orderly lives. Where was a traffic cop when you needed one?

With his mission accomplished, Rickie detached himself and started toward my house.

I grabbed his shoulder. "What do you think you're doing?"

"I told them I wanted to stay with you. I missed you."

I narrowed my eyes and fixed him with a cold stare. "Bullshit. You were so awful, they dumped you on me."

"Whatever." He turned away but I held onto his shoulder and looked at Fred.

"Will Sophie keep him while we're gone?"

"She's still at her shop, trying to get everything set up."

"Paula's not home yet. If you've got some handcuffs, I could lock him in the basement."

"No time. We'll take him with us. Rickie, get in the back seat of my car." Fred motioned toward his white Mercedes.

Without another word, Rickie walked toward Fred's car.

"How do you do that?" I asked.

"Vulcan mind control."

We headed across town and hit road construction. Kansas City highways always have at least one and usually two lanes closed at any given time. During the winter it's due to ice and snow, and during the spring and summer, it's due to construction to repair the damages of all that ice and snow.

Nevertheless, we made it across town and out to the country in record time, thanks to my driving skills and whatever modifications Fred had made to that engine. I prefer my smaller car because it's easier to slip in between other vehicles, but the power in Fred's car made it a good tradeoff.

Of course I didn't get a ticket, not with Fred along to put a protective Vulcan shield around the car.

Following his directions, I drove from the highway to a paved road to a dirt road where I was forced to drive slow, very slow. Even so, we bounced over the rutted road in a way that made my teeth rattle. In the summer drought, the dust enveloped us. Fred would doubtless be up all night washing his car.

"Pull off the road in that clear area." He pointed a couple of hundred feet up the road.

I followed his instructions then looked around. Nothing but trees and weeds. "What's going on? You're not planning to dump the kid here, are you? Not only will we get in big trouble with Social Services, but he'll just follow us back home anyway."

"I'm not getting out in the middle of nowhere," Rickie said. Obviously he was concerned about Fred's plans to dump him.

"We have to walk the rest of the way to the farmhouse," Fred stated emphatically.

"We do?"

"These people are paranoid. The road doesn't go up to their houses. Put on your scarf. You can't let anyone but your husband see your hair."

"All these women have bad hair?"

"It's a sign of submission. We have to blend if they're going to talk to us."

Reluctantly I wrapped the scarf over my head. Just what I needed in the August heat. "What about him?" I nodded to Rickie in the back seat who sat there quietly in his blue jeans and a T-shirt with zombies on it. He wasn't going to blend.

"We'll explain him. Rickie, hand me that box in the seat beside you."

Rickie obediently handed him a rectangular carton about the size of a shoe box. Fred opened it and took out a dead albino creature.

I shuddered. "What are you going to do with that?"

He attached it to his face. A beard. "Think I should grow one?"

"I promise to buy you a lifetime supply of razors if you don't."

We left the air conditioned car and trudged out across the field in the afternoon heat.

Three hours later we arrived at Dr. Dan's home place. Fred said it had been only twenty minutes, pointing to the sun which still occupied roughly the same position in the sky as when we'd left the car, but I figured if he could manipulate Rickie's mind, he could manipulate the sun. I'm sticking with my estimate of three hours for that hot, dirty walk in those stifling clothes.

As we approached the house, I began to comprehend the real meaning of *self-sustaining farm.* If they couldn't build it or grow it themselves, they didn't have it. Whoever built the house might have constructed buildings of Legos in his childhood, but he'd never taken a class in architecture. The porch listed to one side, and the house listed to the other. The wood was rough and desperately needed a coat of paint. The screen on the front door was rusted and torn and sagged from one hinge.

Another building that could be a barn or a guest house crouched nearby. Plants in the vegetable garden on one side of the house were withered and sere in the late summer drought. A drooping clothes line supported several black garments and pairs of overalls ranging in size from small to huge. Kids must live there, but they were not outside laughing and playing.

The yard was closer to my style than to Fred's, and a few chickens wandered around, pecking here and there. As we crossed the yard, I realized the chickens were fertilizing as they went. It meant we had to navigate carefully, but it wasn't a bad idea. Maybe I'd get a few for my yard. Fresh eggs, fried chicken and free fertilizer. But I didn't want to think about how the chicken made its journey from the yard to the frying pan.

Before we reached the porch, the screen door opened and a thin older woman stepped out. She wore clothing similar to my outfit with a utilitarian apron very like the ones Paula and I wore at work except hers didn't have chocolate stains. Her scarf (she had to wear it in the house too?) revealed the roots of steel gray hair pulled back tightly from a face that was a road map of wrinkles coated with sweat. Her dark eyes were tired. "What do you want?" She didn't smile. I wondered if she ever had.

"Are you Esther Jamison?" Fred asked.

"I am."

"I'm Jacob Sommers, this is my wife, Abigail, and our son, Hezekiah."

I heard Rickie's sharp intake of breath at the name Fred had given him, but he remained silent. That Vulcan mind control was an amazing thing.

"Your sons, Daniel and Joshua, asked us to stop by and see you on our way home."

The woman's thin lips parted and her eyes widened in surprise. "Daniel and Joshua? You saw Daniel and Joshua? Are they okay?"

Fred nodded. "We just talked to Joshua today. He's a lawyer. Our son ran away to the city, and Joshua helped us get him back. When Joshua found out we live on a big farm a ways down the road and were going to travel past your house to get home, he asked us to drop by and tell you they're doing fine. Daniel's a doctor. You have grandchildren."

"Grandchildren? Did Daniel marry Sarah?"

Fred shook his head slowly and the beard moved across his chest as if it was alive. Creepy. "No. He didn't marry her."

179

"What about the baby, the little girl?"

The baby. *Carolyn?*

"She died."

Esther's eyes misted and she blinked a couple of times, but this was not a woman accustomed to showing her emotions. "It's just as well. What chance did that poor little thing have without a daddy? What about Sarah?"

"She died too."

Esther nodded. "I'll tell her mother when I see her."

"Has she heard nothing from Sarah in all these years?"

"Of course not. When they leave, they're dead to us."

"I'm sorry to bring bad news."

"No good can come of going out into that world." She shook her head. "I wonder if Matthew knows Sarah's dead? He left home to look for her years ago. He may be dead by now."

Matthew? That got my attention. True, it's a common name, but this wasn't likely a coincidence.

"Who's Matthew?" I asked.

Esther looked at me as if surprised I was able to speak. "Sarah's brother. He was just a little boy when she took her baby and left home to find Daniel. It was rough on her, having a baby with no father. Then Ezekiel offered to marry her after his wife died. He was a lot older, but it was the best she could expect since she had that baby. But she didn't want Ezekiel. She wanted Daniel. I hoped she'd find him and..." Her voice trailed off and she looked away into the distance. Whatever she'd hoped, she knew it hadn't happened. Likely most of her hopes hadn't happened.

An older man with a white beard that looked like it had been dead even longer than Fred's stepped through the door and aimed a shotgun at us. "Who are you people?"

I took that as a sign we were not welcome there and should leave immediately, but Fred introduced us as if social interaction at the end of a gun was perfectly normal. I watched Rickie from the corner of my eye. He made a face at the repetition of his new name but he didn't react otherwise. Was I the only one who thought that crazy man could squeeze the trigger and blow us into the next county at any moment?

"They live on a farm down the road," Esther said meekly. "They brought word from Daniel and Joshua."

The man moved closer to the edge of the porch and lifted the gun higher. He was old...probably not as old as he looked...but he stood tall, and his chest was wide beneath the overalls and dingy white shirt. I would not want to meet him in a dark alley. "I don't know anything about another farm down the road, and Daniel and Joshua are not our sons anymore."

Esther dropped her gaze. A properly subservient wife.

"I didn't know you could divorce your kids." The words just slipped out of my mouth. Shotgun or no shotgun, I was tired of listening to that rude man mouth off.

"You need to control your wife," the man said.

I changed my mind. I did want to meet him in a dark alley. At that moment, I felt sure I could take him down even without my iron skillet.

"Our community allows women to express themselves during the days when the moon is waxing gibbous," Fred said.

The man blinked a couple of times but had no response to that statement.

"We have miles to go before we sleep." Fred turned and strode away.

Rickie followed immediately.

"If we don't get to express ourselves, we've been known to murder our husbands in their sleep." I shot Esther a suggestive glance. "And we alibi for each other."

I yanked off that suffocating scarf, stomped through that yard as if the chicken poop didn't bother me, and hurried to catch up with Jacob and Hezekiah.

"I get it," I said as we walked through the fields, away from Dr. Dan's parents. "Now I understand how two people could disappear off the face of the earth without anybody knowing."

Fred pulled the beard from his face. "Nobody but Sophie, her parents and the murderer."

"I want a Coke," Rickie said.

For once, Rickie and I were on the same page.

Chapter Seventeen

Fred's immaculate car was not immaculate when we got back to it. A thick layer of dust had turned the gleaming white to dusty beige.

"Car's dirty," I said, just to see how he'd respond. I half expected him to freak out.

He gave it scarcely a glance. "It's washable." He unlocked the doors and we all got in.

After sitting in the sun with the windows closed, the car was probably twenty degrees hotter than outside which was already pretty hot.

"Hey, my window won't go down," Rickie complained from the back seat. "There's no handle."

"You're correct. I control the windows." Fred started the engine. "It'll cool down pretty fast. In the meantime, just sweat. I'm sure you know how to do that."

The car did cool down amazingly fast as Fred ambled along the dirt road. Really, that's the only way I can describe his driving. Made me want to open the door, put my foot on the ground and push.

"What do we do now?" I asked. "We know Dr. Dan did it."

"Do we?"

"Who's Dr. Dan?" Rickie asked.

"Nobody you know," I assured the kid, then turned back to Fred. "Okay, we *assume* Dr. Dan did it. Will you go with me on that?"

He nodded. "I will agree that it is possible Daniel did it."

"He ran away from home to go to school, to escape from that house and that grumpy old man. Had a promising life ahead of him. Even married a rich woman so he didn't have to struggle so much to get through med school. But then his past catches up with him. His girlfriend from back home shows up with a baby."

Fred nodded. "That fits with the data. Sarah left the farm and came to find the father of her child. Daniel felt a sense of responsibility, so he tucked her away in an old house in Pleasant Grove where his rich wife and his new friends would never find her. But then something happened."

"What?" Rickie asked.

"That's what we need to figure out," I said. "Maybe the rich wife finds out. Or maybe Sarah wants to get married. With her background, it's got to bother her that she's a single mom. Remember, she did tell the Murrays Dan was her husband."

Fred squinted as he stared through the haze of dust stirred up by his car. I was amazed he could see enough to keep the car on the road. "That's one possible scenario. He killed them, disposed of their bodies, sold the house, and there's no evidence they ever existed. The family back home has already written them off. Who's going to file a missing persons' report? They don't even have birth

184

certificates on file. The doctor is home free, able to live out his dreams and be a physician to the wealthy. No bodies, no murder weapon, no fingerprints, no DNA."

I glanced in the rearview mirror. Rickie was leaning forward, eyes wide, completely absorbed in our discussion. Considering the life he led, I doubted anything we said was going to shock him or give him nightmares so I continued.

"But there was a witness. Sophie saw it happen. She ran out of the closet and Dr. Dan followed her home, probably intending to kill her too."

"That wouldn't be easy with her parents there. Maybe he bribed them to move out of town and keep quiet. Remember the hundred thousand dollars deposited in their account?"

I considered that possibility. "You think he killed them after they moved to Nebraska? Why would he do that if he'd already bribed them?"

"Maybe they changed their minds and were going to talk. Maybe they wanted more money and he couldn't get it without his wife finding out. Maybe their deaths were an accident after all."

I gave a snort of derision. "And Sophie almost died from the same cause after she came back to town. That would be a major coincidence."

"Coincidences do happen. That's why we have a name for them."

He just said that to be argumentative. "Where does Matthew fit into this picture?"

"He left home to find his sister. Esther Jamison knows him and his family which means he knows them. Maybe he tracked down the doctor, found out he owned my house during the time his sister would have been around, and that's why he's checking out the neighborhood."

I wasn't sure what that might mean for his relationship with Paula, but it didn't sound good. "Maybe, maybe, maybe. It's not like you to be uncertain, Fred."

"We have no hard evidence. It's all speculation and conjecture until we get a confession."

"A confession? Really? Any idea how we go about that?"

"Yes, I have a few ideas."

I waited for him to share some of those ideas with me. He didn't.

"Can we have pizza when we get home?" Rickie asked.

Home? A wave of anxiety twisted my gut. He was referring to my house as *home*. What if Grace never came back to get him? What if Rick stayed in Hawaii? Was I going to be stuck with Rickie forever? I could just see myself taking him to school in the fall, going to PTA meetings, picking him up at the gate when he got out of prison.

A loud crash shattered my reverie and I slammed forward against my seatbelt. "What the h... What was that?"

Immediately Fred hit the gas and the car leapt forward, speeding along the dusty, rutted road. Damn! Fred knew how to get that car out of second gear after all.

"What the hell just happened?" Rickie asked. I'd censored my words, but Rickie felt no need to do so, and I didn't feel the need to chastise him at that moment.

"Rear end collision." Fred scowled as he stared intently at the road ahead and continued to accelerate. "Hang on."

We'd been rear ended?

Fred was driving fast?

I didn't know which of the two shocked me more.

I looked through the back window and saw an evil, grinning face...headlights and the huge grill of a black truck bearing down on us. "Holy sh...cow!" It was like a scene out of a horror movie. A demonic machine come to life and attacking the good guys. The truck's windows were heavily tinted, so I couldn't see anybody inside, just the evil vehicle with its toothy grin, determined to kill us.

Rickie followed my gaze. "Who the devil is that?"

I hadn't seen any signs of a truck at the Jamison's place or any way for a truck to get there. Even so, the thought crossed my mind that the driver was Esther's husband. The truck even looked a little like him minus the beard.

"Rickie, why don't you lie down on the floor between the seats?" Fred suggested. He had added seatbelts to the front but not the back.

"I don't want to."

"Lie down between the seats," Fred instructed, and Rickie complied without protest or swear word.

The monster truck loomed larger behind us, and I braced for another collision.

Suddenly Fred spun the car onto pavement, making the ninety-degree turn on two wheels. In spite of being in shock and probably terrified if I had time to think about it, I was impressed with that turn.

And then we were flying. Well, almost. I wouldn't have been surprised if he'd pulled out a secret thruster and we'd gone airborne. I couldn't see the speedometer, but I was pretty sure we were doing over a hundred, and that car was handling the speed with no effort. The engine was still purring along, and the suspension held us securely on the road.

I looked over at Fred. I half expected to find he had morphed into Batman or James Bond. He was still Fred. His jaw muscles looked a little tighter, but for all the strain that showed on his face, he could have been driving calmly down the street, going the speed limit as usual.

When this was over, I was going to demand that Fred tell me where he'd learned to drive like that.

And he, of course, would ignore my question and change the subject.

My cell phone rang. *Out of a Blue Clear Sky*, Trent's ringtone. I snatched the phone out of my purse and had my finger poised to accept the call, but hesitated. I really needed to talk to Trent, to hear his voice and to tell him how I felt about him in case I didn't survive the attack of the monster truck. But he'd be very upset if I told him what was going on. Very, very upset, and there was nothing he could do to help. By the time he got there, we'd either be dead or free.

I put the phone back in my purse. If I lived, I'd call him later and maybe I'd try to be a little more forthcoming with my feelings.

The truck was still behind us, but he was no match for whatever Fred had under the hood combined with Fred's driving skills. I was relieved to notice that we were gaining ground fast. I wasn't sure what was going on, but I was pretty sure we needed to get away from the demon in the black truck...or the demon that was the black truck.

Fred flew around a sharp curve...and kept on curving. He swung onto the shoulder of the road and made a U-turn. We were speeding straight for a head-on collision with the ominous black truck.

My stomach leapt upward into my throat. I could see no good coming of this turn of events. "Uh, Fred, are we going to eject out of the seats at the last minute or something?"

"Relax."

I clutched the edge of the seat and gulped while my heart moved from double time to triple time. "That's not going to happen."

At the last minute the truck swung onto the shoulder of the road, missing us by inches, maybe centimeters. I could feel the hot, sulfurous fumes from its exhaust as we passed. Well, I might have if the windows had been open.

Fred swung onto the opposite shoulder of the road and made another U-turn.

Ahead of us the truck seemed to have a little trouble getting back onto the pavement but made it just before we caught up to him.

Again the chase was on, but this time we were the chaser instead of the chasee.

"Fred?" The word sounded tiny and alone, nothing like my regular voice, but I was pretty sure I was the one who said it.

"Yes?"

"What are you going to do with him if you catch him?"

"Beat him within an inch of his life and make him tell me why he damaged my car."

"Maybe you could call him on his cell phone instead."

"I'm kidding. I only want to get his license number. He doesn't have a front plate. I won't do anything dangerous with the kid in the car."

In all the excitement, I'd forgotten Rickie. I looked in the back. He crouched in the floor between the seats, looking up with no sign of fear. Apparently I was the only one in the car who considered our situation life-threatening.

"Are you okay?" I asked him.

"I need to go to the bathroom."

"Just hold on. We'll be there soon." I wasn't sure where *there* was, but at the speed Fred was driving, we'd be there soon.

I peered through the windshield. "I got his plate number."

"So do I. We'll head home now."

We squealed around another turn and onto the highway with Fred close on the truck's bumper.

"Are we heading home now?" I asked as we continued to try to crawl up the truck's rear end.

190

"This is the way home. As long as we're going this way, we might as well torment this person who damaged my car."

"Or we could do that later. Remember, kid in the car."

Fred smiled. "You're not worried, are you, Lindsay? You're the one who's always trying to make me drive faster." But he eased off the gas and allowed the monster truck to merge into traffic and disappear ahead of us. "You can sit up now, Rickie."

I drew in a deep breath. "Somebody was trying to kill us!"

"I doubt he meant to kill us. Probably just trying to scare us. Dr. Dan must have found out about our visit to his old homestead. I saw that truck darting in and out of traffic on our trip over. You lost him, but he must have figured out where we were going. They shouldn't have done that. Now I'm angry."

He didn't really sound angry, not the way he'd sounded when he'd learned about Rickie's theft of Sophie's ring. He still looked the way he always looked. His white hair was immaculate. His black framed glasses sat squarely on his nose. He wasn't white knuckling the steering wheel or scowling after the bad guys. But I did not doubt for one minute that he was extremely angry, angrier than I'd ever seen him before.

"Are we going home for pizza now?" Rickie asked.

"Yes, we are." I took out my cell phone to order a pizza and remembered Trent's call. He'd left a message. I checked my voicemail.

"Call me when you get a chance. I have information about Matthew Graham."

I wasn't sure at that point he could tell me anything I didn't already know about Matthew, but I'd call him as soon as we got home.

I ordered a pizza to be delivered to my house.

A few minutes later Fred pulled up in his drive. "Doors are unlocked," he said.

Rickie immediately slid out of the back seat and ran toward my house. I made no move to open my door and get out. "What now?" I asked.

Fred kept his gaze straight ahead, didn't look at me. "Sophie's probably home. I want you to get her out of that house. Take her to your house and both of you stay there until I get back. She's probably going to need to spend the night with you."

Sounded like the situation was getting critical. "And where are you going?"

"Over to have a chat with Daniel Jamison. It's time to get that confession."

I had no intention of being left out of that. "You're going by yourself?"

He looked at me and grinned. "I think I'll be all right alone."

I snatched the keys from his ignition. "No, you won't. I'm going with you."

His grin changed to a smirk. "You have a child to take care of."

"Since Sophie's going to be at my house anyway, I'm sure she'd be thrilled to babysit."

We had a staring contest for a couple of minutes. I won, of course. Fred may hold the records in secretiveness, karate kicks and all sorts of other things I don't even know about, but when it comes to obstinacy, that's my specialty.

He let out a long sigh. "I'll call Sophie. You change clothes. Meet me back here as soon as she gets to your house."

"Okay." I opened my door and climbed out.

"Uh, keys?"

I removed the house key from his ring and handed it to him. "You won't need the rest until it's time for us to leave." I smiled and headed toward my house.

"Call Trent back," he shouted after me.

It didn't take psychic ability for him to know Trent had called me. Fred knew what his ringtone was. But it was interesting that he'd taken note of it during all the activity going on at the time. He doesn't miss much.

The pizza delivery man pulled up just as I reached my porch where Rickie waited. I unlocked the door and let him inside while I paid for the pizza. Henry was nowhere in sight. He'd probably left his post at the front door as soon as Rickie came up the steps. But he'd be waiting by his food bowl.

By the time I made it inside, Rickie was sitting on the sofa with a Coke, and the TV was blaring. Sometimes consistency is overrated.

He followed me to the kitchen where I opened the pizza box and put two slices on a plate then handed it to him.

Henry crouched under the table, looking grumpy. I poured some dry food into his bowl and took a slice of pizza for myself then turned and grabbed the back of Rickie's shirt with my other hand as he headed toward the living room.

"Eat in here, please." I figured I had a fifty-fifty chance he'd do as I asked. "Sophie's coming over." He tried to shrug off my hand. "Fred wants you to take care of her this evening. Watch over her. Guard her from danger."

He ceased trying to escape and nodded solemnly. "I can do that."

Wow! I'd found a way to manipulate him.

I dashed upstairs, eating pizza as I went, trying to avoid tripping on the ugly black skirt. I wondered which came first with those people on the farm. Were they grim and unhappy because they wore ugly clothes or did they wear ugly clothes because they were grim and unhappy? In any event, I certainly didn't blame the ones who'd escaped. Poor Sarah. She went from one sad situation to another. I hoped Fred planned to hurt Dr. Dan. I'd hold him down to make it easier.

I changed into a pair of jeans and a T-shirt then went downstairs to find Sophie waiting just inside the front door, her expression solemn. Rickie wasn't in the living room. He was either in the kitchen eating or he'd run away. Either was fine though I had a slight preference for the latter.

"Fred asked me to come over and take care of the boy," she said. "He told me to lock all the doors and windows and to let no one inside. What's going on?"

"It's a long story. We'll have a glass of wine and talk when I get back. Be careful. There's an iron skillet in the kitchen if you need it."

She looked puzzled. "An iron skillet? Do I need to cook something?"

"No, I wouldn't cook in that skillet. Never mind. We'll be back soon. In the meantime, if you see anybody suspicious, call 911."

"We'll be fine." She didn't sound all that sure.

The 911 reference reminded me to call Trent. I hit speed dial as I crossed my yard to Fred's. He was sitting in his car, waiting.

"News about Matthew?" I asked as soon as Trent answered. I didn't want to give him a chance to ask what I was doing. He gets nervous sometimes when I hang out with Fred. I'd tell him about it afterward, when it would be too late for him to protest.

"When Matthew Graham first came to town twelve years ago, he tried to report his sister missing, but he had no proof he ever had a sister. The officer who took the report wrote him off as a nutcase. We were just getting computerized back then, and his case file fell through the cracks."

"Matthew wasn't a nutcase," I said. "His sister lived and probably died in Fred's house."

<u>Chapter Eighteen</u>

Clutching the phone to my ear, I slid into Fred's passenger seat and handed his keys to him.

"We've been for a visit to the not-so-funny farm where Dr. Dan and Matthew grew up," I told Trent.

Fred started the car and we eased down the street. The speed demon I'd ridden with half an hour before was gone.

Trent listened quietly as I told him about the couple from American Gothic and the demon truck that tried to kill us. Actually, he had no choice but to listen quietly as I talked very fast so he didn't have a chance to interrupt. I heard some background noise that was probably cursing, but it's never a good idea to give somebody a chance to talk when you know you're not going to want to hear what they have to say.

Finally I ran out of story.

"You've been busy." Trent sounded a little edgy. "Are you sure you're okay?"

"Absolutely. No harm done except to Fred's car. I was never worried. Fred had it all under control." Okay, maybe that wasn't completely true, but I saw no point in worrying him.

"What are you doing now?" he asked.

"Now? Right now?"

"Right now. This minute. What are you doing?"

I didn't want to lie, but refraining from telling everything you know is different from lying. "I ordered a pizza for Rickie, and I'm just finishing a piece." I put the last bit of crust in my mouth and chewed.

"Rickie? *Rickie?* Don't tell me he's back!"

"Oh, yeah, I forgot to mention that part. The Fergusons brought him over and dumped him. At least they can't accuse me of kidnapping him this time." Though I might have to murder him. The system will probably go easier on me for that.

"What are you going to do with him?"

"I don't know." I didn't like thinking about Rickie, but at least it served to divert Trent from my current activities. "Sophie's at my house and will probably spend the night. Rickie actually seems to like her. Maybe she can keep him from setting off a pipe bomb in my living room."

The traffic light turned green and the jerk behind us, someone even more impatient than I, leaned on his horn.

"Are you talking on your cell phone and driving again?" Trent asked.

"No," I replied truthfully. He didn't ask if I was riding.

"Would you do me a favor?"

"Of course."

"Before you go off with Fred on any more of these expeditions, would you let me know first? I realize Fred's very competent, but I'm a cop. I have a badge and a gun. And I'm your boyfriend. I have a personal interest in your safety. I'd like to be around to take care of you."

Damn. He'd just put me in a tough spot. I didn't want to make a promise I was already in the process of breaking.

"Ask him to come over and spend the night with you," Fred said.

I gaped at him in astonishment. "What? Why?"

"Is that Fred?" Trent asked.

"If things go the way I expect them to," Fred replied, "it won't hurt to have him there to keep you and Sophie safe. And Rickie."

"What?" Sophie, Rickie and I needed protection? "Sophie, maybe, but I have an iron skillet and Rickie's a demon child."

"It's never a good thing when you bring up that skillet," Trent said.

"Trent," Fred said, speaking loudly, "can you come over and spend the night with Lindsay? Things may get rough."

"What is he talking about?" Trent asked.

"I have no idea. But I really would like to see you tonight." There. I'd actually admitted it. I needed him to come over and hold me and tell me everything was going to be all right. I hated to sound needy, but Fred had brought it up. "I have to go now. I'll call you later and we'll talk." I disconnected the call before he had a chance to protest.

I turned to Fred. "What do you mean, things are going to get rough? You're going to make Dr. Dan confess and..." I hadn't thought much beyond that. "You'll subdue him then we'll call the cops and have him hauled in, right? So why did you tell Trent to come over?"

"I don't anticipate that the good doctor will confess immediately. I simply plan to stir him up to the point he's going to feel the need to kill Sophie."

He wasn't smiling. He was serious.

"Oh, well, of course. What a great idea."

"I thought it was."

My phone began to play *Out of a Blue Clear Sky*. I ignored it.

"I'm being sarcastic!" I said. "Are you out of your mind? He's already tried to kill her once!"

"But this time she'll be safe at your house with Trent there to protect her and I'll be waiting for him at Sophie's place. It'll be me he'll try to kill, and that's not likely to happen."

"You're going to pretend to be Sophie? You don't think he'll notice that you're, among other things, a guy?"

"I have a long brown wig."

That was an image I didn't even want to think about. "How are you going to deal with being a foot taller than her?"

"He hasn't seen her up close since she was five years old. We need to table this discussion for later. We're going to be there soon and we haven't even talked about your role in tonight's entertainment."

We were driving through a quiet, opulent area with mature trees, lush green lawns and large homes of indeterminate age, set well back from the street. My mother probably lunched with half the wives in the area.

"Okay, so who am I going to be this evening? Dr. Dan has already met me as a moldy expert."

"It's not so much who you are as how you're going to act. You need to attempt to restrain me, keep me from talking to him and saying too much."

"The Big Mouth of the Midwest is going to try to keep The Enigmatic Man from saying too much? This should be very entertaining."

"I am extremely angry about the damage to my car."

"I understand."

"I am going to express my anger to the doctor and make accusations."

"Fred, I don't know how to tell you this, but you don't do anger convincingly."

"That's his house on the corner."

A sprawling, ranch-style red brick house with a circle drive. Dr. Dan had come a long way from the farm with chickens in the front yard and clothes hanging on the line to dry.

Fred drove up and parked. "Showtime."

He got out of the car and strode boldly to the door. I followed, attempting to match his swagger at first, then wimping out and standing sort of behind him. My mother knew these people. What if she'd showed them pictures of me? Of course, that wasn't likely. I refused to go to Glamor Shots, and she refused to show her friends pictures of me in blue jeans and bare feet with flour on my face.

He rang the doorbell.

The door opened and the blond woman from the photographs on Dr. Dan's desk appeared. Except for her hair style, she looked the same as in the pictures when the children were small. Dr. Dan was good at what he did.

"Dr. Fred Sommers to see your husband."

"I'll tell him. Would you like to come in?"

"No."

Mrs. Jamison blinked rapidly. Fred wasn't following the protocol. She'd invited him into her home and he'd refused.

"I'll get Daniel." She turned and went back into the house, closing the door behind her.

"How to win friends," I said.

"I'm not trying to make friends. I'm trying to make an enemy."

"In that case, good job."

The door opened again and Dr. Dan stood there wearing shorts and a knit shirt. He didn't appear nearly as impressive as he had sitting behind his desk wearing a white jacket. He did, however, have the haughty look of an important man who'd just been disturbed. "I remember you two. You came to my office about some mold in an old house. I thought we settled all that. What do you want?"

"Judging by what just happened to my car, you already know that business about the mold was a lie. This woman isn't a mold expert. She's a special consultant to the Pleasant Grove Police Department, and I'm somebody you don't want to mess with. I don't care about any damn mold. I care about my car." Fred swept an arm toward his damaged Mercedes. He'd used a swear word. He wasn't shouting, but his voice was harsh and angry. If he spoke to me that way, I'd cry. "Do you see what happened to my car?" he demanded. "That vehicle managed to stay in perfect condition for over thirty years and now look at it. It'll never be the same."

Dr. Jamison tried to maintain his haughty look, but fear was rapidly encroaching. "What are you talking about? I didn't do anything to your car."

Fred folded his arms and looked formidable. "Of course you didn't do it yourself. You hired somebody. You wouldn't want to get those country club hands dirty like in the old days when you lived on a farm and wore homemade clothes and had goats and chickens in your yard."

I didn't recall seeing any goats, but that one seemed to hit home anyway. Dr. Dan drew himself up to his full height which was still a couple of inches shorter than Fred. "You need to leave." He turned as if to go back inside the house.

"I got the license number. That truck's registered to Kenneth Murdock, a known drug dealer who's skated on three arrests."

Dr. Dan hesitated.

Fred jabbed me with his elbow. I'd been so fascinated with this unknown side of him, I'd forgotten my role.

I grabbed his arm. "Dr. Sommers, we need to leave."

"I'm betting I'll find out your brother is Kenneth Murdock's lawyer. Did you get him to do a family favor? Does your brother know what you did?"

Dr. Dan turned back toward us, face pale, nostrils pinched, eyes bulging. "If you don't leave immediately, I'm going to call the police."

I tugged at Fred's arm. "Dr. Sommers, let's go."

He yanked his arm away from me. "Why don't you do that, Jamison? Why don't you call the police? They're going to be calling on you soon enough. I don't know if you were trying to scare me or kill me, but stopping me isn't going to keep you out of prison. Sophie goes in tomorrow to look at pictures. She'll identify you as Carolyn's killer, as the man who said *I'm sorry* after he murdered his daughter and the woman who loved him."

Clever, I thought. Tell the man the one small detail then let him assume she remembered the rest.

I would have sworn Dr. Dan couldn't get any paler, but he did. Even with my redhead's skin, I probably looked like George Hamilton in comparison. He opened his mouth as if to speak, but nothing came out.

"What's your wife going to say when she finds out about Sarah and the money you gave her parents to keep their mouths shut? Or does your wife already know? Was she part of it? Was she happy to help you get rid of your mistress and your child?"

"Dr. Sommers," I protested, again tugging on his arm, "this is police business. You shouldn't be telling him."

"Why not? He'll find out soon enough." He got closer, almost nose to nose with Jamison. "I found blood in the floorboards of my bedroom, blood from your daughter. Sophie's testimony will be enough to get a warrant to compel you to give your DNA. We're going to prove that Carolyn was your daughter, that she and Sarah existed and that you killed them. You're going down for a lot more than hiring someone to damage my car."

"Oh, Dr. Sommers, what have you done? He'll run away and hide and we'll never be able to convict him." Yes, it was pretty corny, but I didn't have a lot of time to write and rehearse my lines.

He shrugged off my arm. "He can't hide. I'll find him wherever he goes. It's bad enough you killed your own daughter and her mother, but now you've messed with my car." He pointed a finger at Dr. Dan who flinched as if Fred had hit him. "You're going down. You're going down all the way." Fred turned and strode back to his car.

I followed.

As we pulled slowly away from the red brick ranch, Dr. Dan stood on his front porch watching us. Even in the fading light of the afternoon, I fancied I could see the sheen of sweat on his face.

Fred, on the other hand, was calm and unhurried as always.

"I think you wound him up pretty good," I said. "That was impressive."

"It's our best chance since everything we have is circumstantial. Now we wait for him to go after Sophie. If he doesn't confess, we may never get him for murdering Carolyn and Sarah, but we should be able to get him for Sophie's attempted murder."

"You mean the attempted murder of Fred in a wig. That's really dumb, you know. Let me wear the wig, put on some makeup and we'll have a lot better chance."

He shook his head. "Baiting a murderer is dangerous."

I snorted derisively. At least, I hoped it was derisive and not just disgusting. "When Paula's crazy ex-husband was determined to kill me I got a confession out of him and I'm still alive." But it had been close. That was the first time I'd seen Fred in action. "If things get dicey, you can charge in at the last minute and take him down the same way you took down David. Though I wouldn't mind if you made it the next to last minute instead of the last minute."

He didn't say anything which was better than a refusal.

"I'll make your favorite chocolate chip cookies."

"You'll make those anyway."

If bribery doesn't work, try threats. "I'll hurt your car." He'd seemed genuinely upset that his formerly pristine car had been damaged.

He laughed. "When I bought this car, it had been totaled. I'll just get the same guy who fixed it for me the first time to take care of any damage."

I smacked him on the arm. "You totally lied to Dr. Dan!"

"It was a performance, and apparently a good one if it fooled you after I told you what we were going to do."

I shrugged. "That's no great feat. I'm pretty gullible."

It was getting dark when we pulled into Fred's driveway, but in the moonlight I could see Trent walking up my sidewalk to my front door. Mr. Macho Cop would be horrified if anyone ever referred to him as *beautiful*, but that was the first word that came to my mind...one of the most beautiful sights I'd ever seen.

I slid out of Fred's car and raced over to him, throwing myself into his arms and burying my face against his chest.

He pulled me close and held me tightly. "So you weren't scared at all when the truck tried to run you down?"

"No."

"Not even a little bit?"

"No." I leaned back and looked up at him. "But I'm glad you're here."

"Good evening, Trent. Glad you could make it."

I moved out of Trent's arms and turned to see Fred approaching.

"What's the game plan for tonight?" Trent asked.

"I'm going to wear a wig and pretend to be Sophie," I said.

"No, you're not," Fred and Trent said in unison. Cute.

<u>Chapter Nineteen</u>

"Excuse me? Since when did I give either of you my power of attorney to make my decisions?"

Yeah, my comment made no sense, but it caused both of them to stop and think. It gave me a minute to figure out my tactics.

"So," I said, "you plan to put on a wig and sit in Sophie's house waiting for Dr. Dan to show up and turn on the gas?"

Fred nodded. "Yes."

"He's not an accomplished criminal, you know. He got into her house last time because she left the door open."

"I thought of that. I plan to leave the front door unlocked."

I snorted. "He's going to hang around waiting for Sophie to run across the street to your house so he can slip inside like last time. There's only one way to make this look realistic. I pretend to be Sophie, run out of the house and over to your place to give him a chance to get inside, then you escort me back only this time you don't leave. Dr. Dan will be inside, and you can wait outside with one of your fancy recording devices until you get enough to convict him, then rush in and save me at the next to last minute."

Fred and Trent looked at each other. Trent shook his head. "It's too dangerous."

I rolled my eyes. "I did just fine getting a confession out of David Bennett and you waited patiently outside the whole time."

"That was different. I didn't really know you then. You weren't...we weren't..."

"Lindsay, why don't you go inside and see if Rickie's totally destroyed your place while I talk to Trent."

"I'll go in and pack my overnight bag," I said.

Sophie opened the door as soon as I stepped onto the porch. "I'm glad you're home," she said, concern etched on her features.

Behind her the television was playing, but it wasn't blaring. My first thought was that Rickie had run away from home.

However, as I moved inside, I saw him sitting quietly on the sofa, drinking a Coke.

Sophie closed the door behind me and went over to sit beside him. "Rickie told me about the trip to see those people and about the scary truck." She smiled and brushed his hair off his forehead. It sprang right back.

He smiled up at her. "I was scared."

I sighed. He was practicing his scam artist skills on Sophie, and she was totally falling for it.

"How many Cokes has it taken to make you feel secure?" I asked.

He shrugged. "Three or four."

I went to the refrigerator and got a soda while there were still some left then took a seat in my arm chair. "Here's the game plan," I said. "Fred antagonized Dr. Dan. Told him you've recovered the memory of Carolyn's death and you're going in tomorrow to identify him so they can issue a warrant to get his DNA and compare it to the blood Fred found in his floorboards."

Sophie gasped. "He found blood? Carolyn's blood?"

"No, he made up that part, a fictitious presentation of data."

"Oh."

"So you're going to spend the night here with Rickie and Trent, and I'm going to your house to pretend to be you, pretend to sleepwalk to Fred's and leave the house unlocked, then when Dr. Dan comes to kill you, we'll get his confession. Worst case scenario, we take him down for trying to kill you."

Sophie sat upright, shaking her head vigorously. "No, I can't let you do that! That's dangerous. I'll do it. Fred will be there."

"Yes, Fred will be there, so it won't be dangerous for either of us, but I have skills you don't."

She sat on the edge of her seat, waiting to hear about those skills.

"Do you know karate?" I asked her. "Ju-jitsu? Kung-foolery?"

Her eyes widened and she sat back again. "I had no idea you knew all those martial arts."

"I don't like to brag." Of course I knew nothing about karate and ju-jitsu. I never said I did. I simply asked if she did. As for kung-foolery, maybe I did know something about that.

Trent came in the front door. "All right," he said, "you get to play the part of Sophie but only if you maintain an open line to me on your cell phone the entire time."

I was very curious as to what Fred told him that changed his mind. Perhaps it was a clue to Fred's true identity. But he wasn't likely to tell me with so many people around. I'd ask him when we were alone and he was vulnerable.

"Where's Uncle Fred?" Rickie asked.

"He went home to get ready for tonight," Trent replied.

"And you have to do your part," I added. "Sophie's going to spend the night here and you're going to stay with her and take care of her."

Trent looked startled but Rickie looked solemn. "I can do that."

Sophie smiled and put her arm around his shoulders, pulling his head close to hers. She'd probably get lice.

I ran upstairs to grab a toothbrush and other toiletries. Henry looked up from where he lay warming my bed and gave an inquisitive "meow?"

"Sorry," I said, "but you're on your own tonight. Stay in here and you should be safe. Sophie's coming up later to sleep with you."

I made him move while I put clean sheets on the bed. He resumed his place immediately and I raced back downstairs. Fred was waiting in the living room. He handed me a brown wig in a style very similar to Sophie's.

"You can't wear those clothes," he said. "Jamison saw you wearing those. Change into a white blouse and khaki shorts so you'll look like her. He could already be waiting and watching."

I took the wig then went back upstairs to change from my T-shirt and cutoffs to the requested costume. I was glad Sophie wasn't wearing a ball gown and four-inch heels.

I stood in front of my cheval mirror and donned the brown wig. Hiding all my red curls wasn't easy, but I'd done it before when I'd worn the blond wig. I added some makeup and checked myself in the mirror. Not exactly a Sophie clone, but for somebody who hadn't seen her up close in over twenty years, I could probably pass.

I hurried back to the kitchen where I grabbed a six-pack of Cokes and the leftover half of a Triple Chocolate Mousse Cake. I set the cake in my iron skillet and took both with me. Sure, I trusted Fred and Trent to take care of me, but it never hurts to have a little backup.

"My gowns are in the second dresser drawer," Sophie said.

"My night shirts are in my top dresser drawer." She was probably going to have quite a culture shock.

I gave Trent a kiss and grabbed my purse from the coffee table. Fred took the Cokes from me, and he and I went out the door.

"Call me as soon as you get there," Trent said.

"Walk slowly," Fred directed as we crossed the street. "There's more to this impersonation business than just a wig and khaki shorts."

I slowed my pace and looked up and down the street for any suspicious activity. It was completely dark. The moon hadn't risen yet, and the only streetlight was up the street. Well, there's one directly in front of my house but somebody shot it out with a BB gun a couple of years ago and nobody's replaced the bulb yet. If anybody ever does, I'll shoot it out again. Damn thing shone right in my bedroom window.

When we got to Sophie's, Fred tucked the Cokes under his arm, took out a key and opened the front door.

"Did Sophie give you a key?" I asked.

"Yes. Where else would I have got one?"

I shrugged. "I figured you had some special master key that unlocked all our doors." I moved inside the showplace house.

He laid a hand on my shoulder, and I turned back to face him. "Call me if anything unexpected happens."

Good grief. I couldn't believe he and Trent both thought I was so helpless. "Whatever," I said, using Rickie's favorite word.

He left, and I closed and locked the door behind him.

I put the Cokes and cake in the refrigerator, took a firm grip on the iron skillet then made a tour of the house. I needed to know the layout in case a crazed killer chased me around the place.

Sophie's bedroom was amazing. The ceiling went all the way up to the peak of the roof, and a fan hung down, its blades swirling lazily. The king-sized bed was draped with a down-filled white comforter accented by several brightly colored pillows of various shapes tossed about in a seemingly casual pattern. Her dresser and armoire were antiques, not matching but both made of cherry wood. Her nightstands were round, skirted tables holding lamps with crystal bases which again complemented each other but weren't exact replicas. Everything in the room was elegant and casual at the same time. Inviting and intimidating. Her interior design business was likely going to be a huge success.

I opened the second dresser drawer and found several silky white night gowns. I chose one at random, slipped out of my shorts and shirt and pulled it over my head. Not a bad fit. A little roomy up top, but that was better than being too tight. I was a couple of inches taller than Sophie, so at least I wouldn't trip on it as I ran across the street to Fred's house in our reenactment scene. It actually felt quite nice against my skin. Maybe I would buy a silk T-shirt to sleep in.

I took my cell phone from my purse, flopped backward onto the bed and hit Trent's speed dial.

"Hi, baby," he said.

"I'm lying here all alone in a sumptuous king sized bed, wearing nothing but a silk nightgown. Give you any ideas, sexy guy?"

"Hang on just a minute. Let me take you off speaker phone."

My face got hot. I was pretty sure it had turned the rich shade of a Coke can.

"So you're all settled in?" he asked.

"Yes. You can put me back on speaker phone, then we can both set down our phones and do something else as we wait until midnight when I turn into a sleepwalker."

I turned down the covers and lay back on the bed. It was like lying on a cloud.

A floorboard creaked, and I sat bolt upright.

Stupid. It was an old house. Old houses creaked. Mine certainly did, but I was accustomed to the creaks and groans of my house.

I took my cell phone in one hand and the skillet in the other then tiptoed downstairs and checked all the rooms.

Nobody was there. The doors were locked. I was being silly. However, my motto was, better silly than dead.

I went back to bed, took out my e-reader and read for a while. Finally put my book aside and turned off the light.

"Good night," I said, speaking in the general direction of my cell phone.

"Good night, baby."

I smiled into the darkness. Nice to hear his voice. Nice to know he was there.

I dozed a little. I was tired but too wound up to sleep. The gown was comfortable though it kept wrapping around my legs when I turned over, and that wig was driving me crazy. Every time I moved, I had to adjust it. If Dr. Dan should arrive unexpectedly, I didn't want to look like Ronald McDonald in the middle of a costume change.

And I admit, I was a little nervous. Not scared, just a little nervous at being in a strange house.

I tried to ignore the noises of that house, assured myself nobody could get into the house without Fred or Trent seeing him.

Finally about eleven I gave up, got up and went downstairs. Might as well have some chocolate.

The entire first floor glowed faintly with some sort of ambient lighting Sophie had included in her decorating scheme. I like bright light, so I turned on a regular lamp, then immediately turned it off when I realized I was putting myself in the spotlight. No need to make it easy for Dr. Dan, the killing man.

I went into the kitchen and took the mousse cake out of the refrigerator. Sophie had a beautiful set of knives in a wooden block. I chose the largest chef's knife, cut myself a generous piece, put it on a dessert plate and took it to the living room.

I took a bite. It was delicious. Went a long way toward soothing my nerves. I barely jumped when I heard a noise at the back door. Probably a raccoon or a possum.

About the third bite, my phone began playing *Out of a Blue Clear Sky*. The fact Trent was calling meant we'd lost our connection somewhere in the course of the last couple of hours. Blasted cell phone service. Good thing I hadn't needed him.

I hit the icon to accept the call. "What's up?"

"Nothing. Absolutely nothing. The whole thing's off."

"What? No!"

"Sorry I had to hang up on you, but I got a call from the station. Jamison's in the hospital. Took an overdose. Tried to commit suicide."

"Well, I guess Fred succeeded in scaring him. I don't suppose he left a note confessing to everything."

"No such luck. He went upstairs after dinner and locked himself in his office. He does that a lot, and his wife only became concerned when she got a call from his brother saying Daniel wasn't answering his cell phone. She found him slumped over his desk and called 911."

"Is he going to live?" If he died by his own hand without ever confessing to the evil he'd done, at least he'd no longer be a threat to Sophie. But it would be less satisfying than seeing him go to trial and be punished for his crimes.

"They got to him in time. Son of a bitch will live. I'll question him as soon as he's conscious, but I doubt he'll admit to anything."

My heart plummeted. All our hard work had blown up in our faces. "Damn! And now he'll know we were lying about Sophie making an identification or Fred having blood for DNA comparison. Damn, damn, damn!"

"We'll figure out something else. Come on home. I already told Fred. I'll let you wake Sophie when you get here so the two of you can exchange houses."

"Will you stay the night?" Again I hated to sound needy, but I was feeling kind of needy.

"Yes, I'll stay the night. I'll leave before Rickie gets up in the morning."

"I'll clean up my mess, change clothes and be right there."

"I'll be waiting for you."

I disconnected the call and sank back against the sofa cushions, suddenly exhausted. I'd been running on adrenalin, excited about taking down a murderer, avenging the death of a little girl, keeping Sophie safe. Now I was just tired.

I heard a noise at the back door again, but I didn't even flinch. The bad guy was in a hospital room with nurses waiting on him hand and foot, doctors exerting every effort to keep a worthless piece of scum alive. I was not concerned with the creatures of the night or the creaks and groans of an old house.

I leaned forward, retrieved my plate and took another bite. When life throws a curve ball, eat chocolate.

I heard a faint scratching at the front door. I didn't have enough energy to get concerned. It could be anything, maybe even Henry. If Trent or Sophie had let him out of the house, he'd likely come to find me.

The front door whispered open.

That did get my attention. Henry, possums and raccoons didn't open doors.

I stood, still clutching my plate of chocolate mousse, and looked in the direction of the door. "Trent?" I asked hopefully.

217

The tall man dressed in black and wearing a ski mask was definitely not Trent. Dr. Dan must have been released from the hospital already.

"You!" we exclaimed at the same time.

We were both wrong.

Chapter Twenty

He dropped the can of gasoline he was carrying and charged across the room toward me. For an instant I was paralyzed with horror. But only for an instant. Still clutching my plate of mousse, I ran away from him as fast as I could, though the length of my strides was hampered by the width of that beautiful but impractical gown.

I made it to the kitchen doorway when a hand grabbed my shoulder, stopping me in my tracks.

I admit it. I was scared. This was not part of the plan. I'd left my iron skillet upstairs. All I had was a piece of half-eaten chocolate mousse cake. Putting my life in the hands of my chocolate, I whirled around, yanked off his ski mask with one hand and smashed the remnants of my mousse into his face with the other. A part of my brain registered that he looked different, but I didn't have time to think about it.

He let go of my shoulder, and I made a mad dash for the front door.

He bellowed a few curse words and started after me. I'd have made it, but that damn gown got in the way. I stumbled as I rounded the coffee table, and he tackled me from behind. I went down hard, my face smashing against the beautiful hardwood floor. I was pretty sure my nose was broken. It hurt.

His weight settled onto my back and he grabbed one of my arms, pinning it behind me. I returned a few of his curse words. I wasn't ready to die. What would Henry do without me? Who'd make chocolate to help all those people get through their day? And then there was Trent. I hadn't had a chance to tell Trent how I felt about him.

Begging for my life probably wasn't going to work. It never did in the movies. I was in no position to threaten. Logic was all that was left. "Killing me won't help you now, Daniel Jamison," I shouted. "We know who you are and what you've done!"

The man was still for a moment, then he laughed. "You think I'm Daniel? Interesting. You were young when you saw me. I guess to a kid we looked alike. This is all his fault, but I'm not him. He's in the hospital. Tried to kill himself. If you know so much, I'm surprised you don't know that."

I realized then that the voice was different. Similar but different. I tried to twist around to get a better look at him. The blasted wig caught as I turned and I could feel it sliding.

"What the devil?" He grabbed the wig and yanked it off.

"I was having a bad hair day." I could see enough to verify that he wasn't Dr. Dan. He looked a lot like him but his face was thinner, harder. And dotted with chocolate mousse.

But what really got my attention was the hypodermic needle in the hand that held my wig. I wasn't sure what was in that hypodermic, but I'd be willing to bet he wasn't planning to give himself an insulin injection.

"You have red hair?" He looked at the wig then at me. "I don't remember red hair."

I could have told him I wasn't Sophie, but at that point I didn't think it would make any real difference. "It was an accident. I was trying to add highlights."

He bit his lip and cursed. "You were supposed to be asleep. This would have been so easy if you'd been upstairs asleep. I'm not a murderer! I don't like being forced to do this."

"Jay?" I guessed. "Dr. Dan's brother?"

He gave a short, ugly bark, something between a laugh and a snort. It was not a pleasant or reassuring sound. "Yeah, the doctor's brother. I thought this was over, all behind me. Why couldn't you just stay gone? Daniel paid your family to stay gone."

"He paid them but then he killed them. They— we moved to Nebraska, but your brother killed my parents."

"Not him. Never my perfect, upright, uptight brother. They died because your father was as much a prig as my brother. Your father couldn't live with the guilt. He was going to give back the money and tell the police what I'd done. I had to get rid of them. I had no choice."

For a moment I actually felt elation. I did it! I got his confession, though there was nobody around to hear it except me and I might not live to tell anybody. That thought pretty much dampened my elation. "Why did you kill Carolyn? She was just a little girl. She was my friend."

"I had no choice," he said again. "My idiot brother was going to leave Natalie and marry Sarah."

"He loved her and Carolyn. He wanted to do the right thing."

Jay snorted. "The right thing for who? Who'd have benefited from that? Nobody. He was going to give up everything…the big house, nice car, plenty of money. Drop out of school to take care of his family." He made *family* sound like a curse word. "He might as well have stayed at home in the first place."

Maybe if I could focus his anger on that family instead of me, I could talk him out of killing me. "I understand. You escaped from that awful place. He was helping you get through school so you could both have a better life. And she was going to ruin it."

"Daniel went out of his way to take care of her and provide a home for her when she showed up with that kid she said was his. But when she told him she was pregnant again, he was going to throw away everything and marry her. I liked living in a nice house and driving a new car and eating steaks. I liked the opportunity to have a better life. I tried to reason with him, but he wouldn't listen."

"The only logical thing you could have done was kill Sarah and Carolyn and buy my parents' silence."

He heaved a long sigh. "Your parents were a problem. They were going to the cops no matter how much money my brother offered them. But when I threatened to kill you, that did it. I guess since they only had one kid, they worried about that kid. Not so much when you have plenty of spares like my parents." He laughed at his own sick joke.

"What did you do with Sarah and Carolyn after you killed them?"

"The Missouri river was flooded. We cut them up and dumped them."

I shuddered at the casual way he sounded as he described the macabre deed. He had no soul. With a sinking feeling I realized he was not going to let me live no matter what I said or did. He was going to inject me and watch me die without a second of remorse.

My only chance was to keep him talking. If I could delay long enough, maybe Trent would realize I was taking too long and would come after me. Maybe Jay would have a heart attack and die. Maybe the New Madrid fault would finally give and we'd have an earthquake and the ceiling would fall on Jay. "Dr. Dan butchered his own daughter and pregnant girlfriend?"

"He did it to help me. I'm his brother. She was just the slut who was going to ruin his life."

Dr. Dan wasn't a psychotic killer. He was a weak man who wanted to help everybody…Sarah, Natalie, his brother…Sophie? "He tried to warn her—me, didn't he? He's the one who called and told me to leave town."

Jay snorted again. "Yeah, he thought that stupid phone call and that doll of Carolyn's would scare you away. I knew better. When I found out the man who lives in Sarah's old house went out to talk to my parents, I knew I had to stop things before it was too late, before you remembered." He tossed the wig aside and took a firmer grip on the hypodermic. "The gas leak would have been a painless death. If you'd been asleep tonight, I'd have given you this shot and you'd have died peacefully. I did my best to make this easy on you, but you've left me no choice."

I thought I heard a sound from the vicinity of the kitchen door. Jay didn't seem to notice, so maybe I was hearing what I wanted to hear.

Or maybe Fred with his x-ray vision and psychic abilities had come to rescue me. Or Trent with his cop skills. Or, better yet, both of them.

I focused on keeping Jay talking and myself drug-free.

"Actually, you do have a choice. Let's sit down and talk about this. We can have a Coke and some more of that chocolate mousse and I'm sure we can figure out something." Something that didn't involve my death.

He laughed. "I'm a lawyer. I know what would happen if I let you live. The whole story would come out. I killed twenty years ago so I wouldn't have to give up the good life, so I wouldn't have to go home. Going to prison would be like going back to that God-awful place where I grew up. I won't do it."

He pressed the needle against my thigh. I gulped and took in a deep breath, maybe my last.

The needle burst through the silk and pricked my skin. I hate shots. I gave as big a lurch as I could under the circumstances. It wasn't much, but it was enough to unsettle him briefly and dislodge the needle from my body.

He cursed again and tightened his hold on my arm, pulling it back painfully and twisting me so my nose hit the floor again.

"Son of a bitch," I shouted, not bothering to censor my language. "You broke my arm!"

"Stop being a baby. Your arm's not broken. That would look suspicious. I need you to be intact and breathing when the house burns so you'll inhale smoke and it will look like a natural death."

"How am I going to breathe in smoke when my nose is broken and you're going to shoot me up with poison?"

"This isn't poison. It's a heavy duty sedative that will put you to sleep."

"I don't want to go to sleep. Tell you what, how about you let me go and I promise I'll never say a word to anybody about all this."

He laughed. For an instant I thought my reputation for telling everything I knew had reached even him, but then I remembered that he thought I was Sophie. He was just being generically disbelieving.

Again I felt the needle pressing against my thigh. I tried to move, to dislodge him again, but he held my arm so tightly, pressed me so firmly against the floor, I was doing good to breathe. I braced myself. At least he'd promised I'd die peacefully.

"Let her go!"

Jay's hold on my arm eased. I turned my head and saw Rickie standing over us, wielding the knife I'd used to slice the mousse. It still had remnants of chocolate on it. I wanted to laugh and cry.

The kid threw himself on Jay, and Jay fell on top of me, again smashing my nose to the floor.

A large knife, chocolate mousse, a crazy kid and a hypodermic needle full of a heavy duty sedative…we were all going to die.

Something sharp came down on my shoulder. I'd been stabbed!

Suddenly the weight rolled off me. I twisted to see Rickie and Jay grappling. Rickie still had the knife, but he wouldn't for long. He didn't stand a chance against the bigger, older man. I was going to have to save him and then I'd never get rid of him.

I scrambled to my feet.

"Police! Let the boy go!" Trent! He'd save me from Jay!

"Give me the knife." Fred! He'd save me from Rickie!

Jay rose slowly and Fred took the knife from Rickie.

"That man stuck a needle in my leg." Rickie indicated his thigh where he had so many mosquito and chigger bites, a small needle prick was not easily perceived.

Trent stepped forward and shoved his gun into Jay's face. "What did you give the kid?"

Jay glared. "I want a lawyer."

Trent pulled back the hammer of his .38. "I'm already pissed at you for attacking my girlfriend. I'd love to have an excuse to blow your brains out."

"I didn't give that kid anything. It was a mild sedative. If he got any of it, he'd be asleep by now."

I held up the empty hypodermic. "It went somewhere."

Trent shoved his gun into its holster and slapped handcuffs on a sullen Jay then examined his own hands. "What is that sticky stuff?"

"Chocolate mousse."

Trent finally turned his attention to me and went quite pale. "You're bleeding. Did he hurt you?"

"Duh! Threw me on the floor and broke my nose, maybe my arm, and then stabbed me in the back! I hope you're going to avenge me."

Trent turned me around and studied my back. "You haven't been stabbed and your arm isn't broken, but that nose does look pretty bad. I'll see to it that he goes away for the rest of his life. How's that?"

"Not as satisfying as it would be if you'd punch him in the nose right now."

"You know I can't do that."

There are definite downsides to having a cop for a boyfriend. If he'd been a gangster, he wouldn't have hesitated to beat the guy to a pulp.

I stepped forward and drew back my fist. "Maybe you can't, but I can."

Trent grabbed my hand. "No, you can't, not when he's in the custody of a police officer."

I looked at Fred. He shrugged and brought me a tissue. Two strong men and nobody was going to avenge my broken nose?

I glared at Jay. "I know people. You'll be looking over your shoulder for the rest of your life. When you least expect it—" I slammed one fist into the other meaningfully. He didn't look very frightened.

Fred put an arm around me. "Let's get both of you to the emergency room, have Rickie checked and your nose taken care of."

Rickie came up on my other side and wrapped a skinny arm around my waist. "Does it hurt much?"

"Yes. Does it hurt where he gave you a shot?"

"No."

"Do you feel sleepy?"

"No."

Across the room a million miles away Trent guarded his prisoner. "Thanks for taking them, Fred. I'm sorry, Lindsay. I've got back-up on the way. As soon as somebody else gets here, I'll meet you at the emergency room."

Definitely a few downsides to having a cop for a boyfriend.

ॐॐ

Rickie got checked first at the hospital in spite of the fact that I was the one who was bleeding. They were worried he'd been poisoned and was going to pass out at any minute. I knew better. That kid was tough.

"Are you his parents?" the young doctor asked.

"No," Fred and I said at the same time.

Rickie sat on the cold steel table looking so pitiful that I felt sorry for him even though I knew it was all an act. But he had tried to save my life. "I'm sort of his..." I gulped. "His step—" I gulped again— "mother."

Fred gasped.

Rickie smiled.

I groaned inwardly. Was this like the common-law marriage thing where, if you told enough people you were married, it became true?

The doctor examined Rickie and decreed that he seemed fine. "If he was injected with a sedative, it must have been a small amount. He's showing no signs of it. Keep an eye on him tonight. Wake him up every hour. If you can't wake him up, bring him back in."

I personally thought the kid had received the full dose and was just so hyper, it only made him a little calmer than usual. He hadn't broken any of the instruments in the examining room. That pretty much proved my theory.

Rickie and Fred stood by while the doctor examined my nose.

"You'll be fine," he said. "Take some aspirin and put an ice bag on your nose tonight. If the swelling doesn't go down in a few days, contact your regular physician."

That was it? I was attacked by a murderer, thrown to the floor, got my nose broken, threatened with death, and that guy thought aspirin and an ice bag would make everything all right?

Trent and Sophie met us as we walked out of the hospital and into the summer evening. She rushed to Rickie, and Trent came to me, wrapping me in a big bear hug. I felt a little better.

"I'll take the kid home with me," Fred offered. "Somebody has to check on him every hour, and Lindsay needs to get some rest."

"No," Sophie said, holding Rickie's hand and smiling down at him. "Let him spend the night with me."

Rickie clutched her hand tightly. "I want to go with her, not you."

Sophie did the ineffectual hair smoothing thing again. "You're my hero." She looked at me. "And you're my hero too. I'm so sorry you had to go through this horrible nightmare."

"It was no big deal." I touched my nose and tried to look brave.

"It was a very big deal. I'm deeply indebted to all of you for finding the man who murdered my parents and my friend. I can't tell you how much this means to me."

"Now maybe you won't have nightmares and end up in Fred's house in the middle of the night." I watched her carefully to see if she'd blush or look secretive, like maybe she planned to go back to Fred's house in the middle of the night when she wasn't sleepwalking.

She laughed softly and gave Fred a meaningful look. Or maybe it was a meaningless look. It was hard to tell with my eyes swollen half-shut. "Yes, I think Fred will once again be free from my uninvited nightly visitations."

That was an ambiguous statement. *Uninvited* as opposed to *invited*?

Fred smiled at her. "And you should also be free of uninvited nighttime visitors. No more gas leaks or men with hypodermic needles."

"Nevertheless, I think I'm going to look into getting a security service."

I waited for Fred to offer to help her set up something since he'd done it for his own house.

"I think that's an excellent idea," he said.

Good grief. Did I need to have a talk with him about the facts of life?

"I am so lucky to have such wonderful neighbors. Next weekend we're going to have steaks and champagne at my place."

"Can we go now?" Rickie had been quiet so long I'd almost forgotten about him. He'd definitely got a hefty dose of sedative.

"Yes," Sophie said. "Let's go home and get you to bed."

"Have you got bugs at your house?"

"No, but I have ice cream."

"You can ride with me." Fred draped a casual arm about her waist and she smiled up at him.

Ahhh.

Trent slid an arm about my waist. "And you can ride with me."

Fred, Sophie and Rickie walked off toward his car, and Trent and I went to his. He opened the door for me then leaned over to give me a kiss.

I pulled back. "Oh, no!"

"What? The onion on my burger at lunch? That was over twelve hours ago!"

I smiled. "I'd kiss you right after you'd eaten raw garlic. No, it's Matthew."

"What about Matthew? He had nothing to do with the murder. He was only about ten years old when it happened."

"I know. He came here trying to find his sister. He deserves to know what happened to her."

"I have no doubt you'll take care of that."

"I will. But what worries me most is that Paula doesn't know why Matthew came here."

"So? You can tell her."

"You don't get it. He had an ulterior motive when he met her, a hidden agenda."

"And now he doesn't."

"But he did, and Paula doesn't deal well with dishonest people. She had enough of that when she was married to Zach's sperm donor."

"She likes Matthew, and he seems like a good guy. It'll be all right."

"I'm not so sure."

"You can worry about Paula tomorrow. For what's left of tonight, you need to relax and let me take care of you."

"I don't need to be taken care of. All I need is a couple of aspirin and an ice bag." I didn't mean it, of course. I wanted to be cared for, pampered, babied. But it had to be against my wishes or I'd sound like a wimp.

"In that case I'll fix you a cup of hot chocolate and spend the night with you because I don't want to drive home so late. You'll be doing me a favor if you let me stay with you."

"Okay, that'll work."

I was feeling better about things as I slid into Trent's car. The murders of Sophie's parents as well as Carolyn and her mother had been solved. Nobody would be trying to kill Sophie anymore. Jay would go to prison for the rest of his life or, depending on his lawyer, at least a portion thereof. Dr. Dan would be charged as an accessory.

The guy I...I cared a lot for was by my side and was going to stay there for a few hours. The night was warm with a starry sky and a full moon. Overall, things were good even though I was still stuck with keeping Rickie for a while and could only hope my big mouth hadn't made me his common-law stepmother.

Chapter Twenty-One

I walked into Death by Chocolate the next morning with two black eyes and a swollen nose. At least it was impossible to see the bags I doubtless had under my eyes from lack of sleep.

"Omigawd!" Paula looked up from the gravy she was stirring. "What happened to you?"

"You should see the other guy."

"The other guy? Who? Rickie?"

"No. Jay Jamison. And he's way worse off. He's in jail." I gave her the details of the evening's events.

She stirred the gravy and looked skeptical. "So Rickie came to your rescue?"

"Yeah, sort of. He said he couldn't sleep and was worried about me so he climbed out his window and came over to check on me. I think he was just doing his normal Rickie routine and prowling around. But he did pretty much save my life, especially since Trent heard him when he jumped out of the tree so he called Fred, and the two of them surrounded us. Fred came in the front door and Trent came in the back."

"How did Rickie get the back door of Sophie's house unlocked in the first place?"

"I have no idea. He swore it was unlocked when he got there. It wasn't. I checked it before I went up to bed. Besides, I heard him scratching, trying to get

234

it open. Jay picked the lock on the front door to get in. I can only assume Rickie picked the back door lock. It seems locks only keep out honest people with no lock-picking skills or equipment."

Speaking of honest people—

"We have to talk about Matthew."

She set the gravy off the stove and laughed. Her eyes twinkled. "Okay, okay, you were right. I admit it. He seems pretty special."

"Well, yeah, I think he is, but there are a few things you need to know about him."

Her eyes stopped twinkling and her smile disappeared. "Like what?"

"He's Sarah's little brother. He came to town looking for her." I told her about the conversation Fred and I had with Esther Jamison.

She took a pan of biscuits out of the oven and set them on the counter. Never by word or gesture did she indicate that she was upset except for the noticeable tension in her shoulders and her slightly jerky movements.

"So," I concluded, "we can tell him what happened to his sister and he can put that all behind him, then you and he can see what happens with your relationship."

She moved the biscuits from the pan to the warming oven, again with the jerky movements.

"Right?" I asked. "It's not like he lied to you. He just didn't tell you everything. That's not the same thing at all." I used that rationalization myself quite often.

"No," she said stiffly.

Strictly speaking, that meant she agreed with me that omission wasn't the same thing as lying. But I could tell from the way she spit out the word that she wasn't agreeing with me. That small, two-letter word contained at least two pages of bad words and condemnations.

She took the first pan of cinnamon rolls from the oven and moved all around the kitchen without looking at me.

My best course of action, I decided, was to keep my mouth shut and get busy making chocolate. She would have several hours to think about it all before Matthew got there. I hoped that would be enough.

Just to be sure Matthew came as usual, I waited until we were busy serving breakfast, found Paula's cell phone and texted him that she wanted to see him. He texted back that he would be there and added a smiley face. I hoped he'd still be smiling after he talked to her.

ॐ

The day was winding down and I'd answered at least a million questions (figuratively, not literally) about my face when Matthew came in.

Paula disappeared into the kitchen.

I greeted him at the counter. His eyes widened and he blinked a couple of times when he saw me. I was getting used to that reaction.

"Long story," I said. "I have news about your sister."

His eyes got even wider.

"Yes," I said, "I know who you are and why you came here."

"Does…?" He looked at the kitchen door where the back of Paula's dress had last been seen.

I nodded.

"Is she…?"

I nodded again.

He sighed. "I met her because I was looking for Sarah, but that has nothing to do with how I feel about her."

"I understand. As soon as I tell you about Sarah, I'll take you back to the kitchen and you can see if you can talk sense to her."

"Sarah's dead, isn't she? Daniel killed her, didn't he?"

"She's dead, but he didn't kill her. It was his brother." I gave him an overview of the events of the night before.

Matthew's eyes brimmed with tears. "I knew she was dead but I kept hoping. She was my only sister. There were so many kids by the time I came along, Sarah helped raise me. She was more of a mother than my real mother. I hated all of them for the way they treated her after she had the baby. Then they tried to marry her off to that old man and she had to leave. I was the only one she told. She knew I wouldn't try to stop her. She said she'd send for me as soon as she could. But she never did."

"She would have." I had no way of knowing that, but it seemed the right thing to say.

He nodded. "I know. She wrote me letters after she left home. My mother hid the letters until the day I told her I was going to look for Sarah. Sarah loved that jerk, Daniel. She thought he loved her and was going to marry her, she'd send for me and we'd be one small, happy family." He smiled weakly. "As opposed to the big, unhappy family she was born into."

I put my hand over his. "He did love her. He was going to divorce Natalie and marry her."

He arched an eyebrow. "If he'd done that when she first went to him, she'd still be alive and so would my little niece."

"Daniel loved her. He's just a weak person. What he and his brother did can't be undone, but they will be punished. And you've got to let it go and move on with your life."

He lowered his head and rubbed his eyes, then finally looked up and nodded.

"Whenever you're ready," I said, "you can go talk to Paula."

He stood and squared his shoulders. "I'm ready."

I opened the kitchen door and let him pass through.

"Can we talk?" he said.

"I'm really busy." Paula's voice dripped ice cubes.

I checked the restaurant. The two remaining people were eating. I could spare a few minutes for eavesdropping. It was the only way I'd ever know what was going on. Not like either one of them was going to tell me.

Then the bell over the front door tinkled and my chance to eavesdrop went right down the tube.

A small woman with bright red hair teased and sprayed within an inch of its life walked inside. She wore eyelashes and fingernails that obviously came from Wal-Mart and a pair of cutoffs that had been cut off a couple of inches too much. Grace. Rickie's mother.

A tall, thin man with slicked back brown hair and a beard came in behind her. He was wearing camouflage. My first thought was that Grace had come to accuse me of kidnapping her son, and the guy was a cop. On second thought, it was probably her new husband.

He looked like he could be mean. I edged away from the kitchen door, my gaze searching the room for any potential source of help. The other people didn't even look up from their food.

"Oh, my goodness! You look just terrible!" Grace darted across the room toward me. She's a hugger. I backed as far away as I could. She reached the edge of the counter and stopped, regarding me with that *bless her heart* expression. "Trent told me what happened last night. Don't worry. I broke Rick's nose once, and it healed just fine."

I would have liked to have seen that. "I appreciate the reassurance. So, are you back from your honeymoon?"

"Yes, we are, and I just want to tell you how grateful I am to you for keeping Rickie, Jr., so Chuck and I could enjoy our honeymoon."

The man I assumed was Chuck moved up next to her, and I saw Rickie behind him.

"Chuck, this is Lindsay, the one I told you about that makes all those wonderful cookies."

Chuck nodded but didn't smile. "Pleased to meet you, Lindsay."

Rickie sidled up to the counter. Before he could even ask, I handed him a cookie then took out two more for Grace and Chuck. I had no idea why they were there or what they wanted, but giving them chocolate couldn't hurt.

"Why, thank you," Grace said. "Chuck, we should of got her to make our wedding cake. Becky Carol made it, and it was really dry."

"Gosh, had I only known, I'd have been happy to make you a big, dense chocolate cake."

"Maybe for our first anniversary party." She looked at Chuck and giggled. He smiled down at her. A man of few words. That was probably a good thing considering how much Grace talked. "Rickie just had to come say good-bye. He said you took such good care of him after his worthless daddy dumped him on you."

I forced myself to smile. "We had a great time together." I wasn't sure what he'd told her, but I wasn't going to volunteer anything. I'd already been accused of kidnapping. Child endangerment probably wasn't far down the list after the events of the night before. It doesn't look good for a cop's girlfriend to be charged with those things.

"Say good-bye, Rickie," Grace ordered.

"Bye," he mumbled.

"Wait! Let me give you some cookies to take with you." I reached inside the case, took out all the leftover cookies and put them in a bag. Fred would just have to do without for one day. Getting rid of Rickie was worth foregoing a few cookies. "And some brownies." I added the nutless and nutted versions and handed the bag to Rickie.

"Say thank you, Rickie."

"Thank you," he mumbled.

I reached across the counter and touched his cheek. "You're welcome," I said.

He shrugged. "Whatever."

"I'll let you know the next time we need a babysitter," Grace said, and the three of them turned to leave.

Oh, great.

As they walked out the door, I realized Trent had been standing behind them.

"Hey!" I gave him a genuine smile. "Sorry, I'm fresh out of cookies and brownies, but you can have the baker if you'd like."

A wide grin stretched his lips as he strolled over. Green fire danced in his dark eyes, a sign he was happy. "I'd like." He leaned across the counter and gently touched my face. "How are you doing?"

"Good. No worries. I just became childless again. With Rickie out of my house and my mind, I can deal with a little thing like a broken nose. I take it you had something to do with reuniting the happy family."

"As a matter of fact, I did. I asked Fred to use his talents to find Grace and Chuck."

"Really? You asked Fred? Weren't you afraid he'd do something illegal?"

Trent nodded, and the green in his eyes ramped up a notch. "I *knew* he would. But I figured it would be worth it. Another night with Rickie, and you'd have been the one climbing out your bedroom window to escape. I figured my lieutenant would cut me a little slack if I got involved in a slightly shady activity in the name of love."

Oh, God! He said it again! "So where did he find the happy couple? I assume it wasn't far away."

"Turns out they've been half an hour from here the whole time. They were staying at the Fin and Fur Lodge out by the lake. The newlyweds were getting in a little fishing and hunting."

"Hunting? Deer season doesn't start for three months."

"Rabbits and squirrels."

"Well." I didn't even want to think about that. "At least they won't go hungry."

"And they'll have plenty of dessert. That was a nice thing you did, giving them enough cookies and brownies to keep Rickie on a sugar high for a week."

"Two days at most. He's tough."

He arched an eyebrow and his grin widened. "You say that like you almost admire him."

I snorted. "You're giving me way too much credit."

The last customers came up to pay. Trent waited while I rang up the sale.

"Where's Paula?" he asked when the door tinkled behind the couple.

"In the kitchen with Matthew."

He flinched. "Any explosions or sounds of pots and pans hitting the wall?"

"No, Paula's the silent and deadly type. The quieter it is, the worse things are going."

We listened to the silence for a few seconds.

"Sounds bad," he said.

"Yeah."

Matthew came through the kitchen door. He wasn't smiling. He turned back inside. "I've been trying to find my sister for twelve years. I don't give up easily on the people I care about." He saw us watching and smiled weakly.

"Good luck," I said.

He nodded. "Thanks."

"Hang in there." I tilted my head toward Trent. "Took me a couple of years to catch him. He was worth the wait."

Matthew's smile became a little more genuine. "She's worth the wait too."

"Yes," I said. "She is. I'll talk to her."

He nodded. "Thanks."

Not that I thought anything I said to Paula would make any real difference. She's stubborn. But that wouldn't stop me from trying.

Matthew left, and Trent and I were alone except for the seething woman in the kitchen.

"I guess I'd better go so you can clean up and get home."

"I guess. I should have time for a nap before you get off work. If you wanted to come over tonight, even though it's a work night, I could express my appreciation for your deigning to work with Fred to get rid of the kid."

He nodded slowly. "How do you plan to express that appreciation?"

I shrugged. "How about some Triple Chocolate Mousse Cake?"

243

"That's a start." He gave me a quick kiss and turned toward the door. I'd see him in a few hours. Spend the night with him. Have a chance to talk to him and tell him how much it meant to me that he would join forces with Fred and do something slightly shady in order to help me. Tell him how much I cared for him.

Unless one of us got killed in a car wreck or shot by a madman in the next couple of hours.

"Trent—"

He paused at the door and looked back.

I opened my mouth and tried to say something meaningful, tried to put into words...a word...my feelings for him. I swallowed, cleared my throat and tried again. "See you tonight."

He smiled. "Count on it."

THE END

Read on for more of Lindsay's favorite recipes!

Triple Chocolate Mousse Cake

With thanks to my friend and classmate, Carolyn Hathcote!

Grease with butter a 9 inch spring form pan at least 3 inches high. If desired, line bottom with parchment. Preheat oven to 325 degrees.

Make layers in order.

Bottom Layer:
6 tablespoons butter
7 ounces bittersweet chocolate (60% chocolate)
2 teaspoons vanilla extract
4 large eggs, separated
1/3 cup packed brown sugar, crumbled to remove lumps

Melt butter and chocolate in large bowl in microwave in two 30 second segments, stirring after each. Allow mixture to cool slightly, about 5 minutes. Whisk in vanilla and egg yolks. Set aside.

Beat egg whites at medium speed until frothy. Add half of brown sugar and beat until combined, about 15 seconds. Add remaining brown sugar and beat at high speed until medium soft peaks form.

Fold beaten egg whites into chocolate mixture. Transfer batter to prepared spring form pan, smoothing top.

Bake until cake has risen, is firm around edges, and center has just set but is still soft (center of cake will spring back after pressing gently with finger), 13 to 18 minutes. Transfer cake to wire rack to cool completely, about 1 hour. (Cake will collapse as it cools.) Do not remove cake from pan.

Middle Layer:
2 tablespoons cocoa powder
5 tablespoons hot water
7 ounces bittersweet chocolate (60% chocolate)
1-1/2 cups cold heavy cream
1 tablespoon sugar
dash salt
1/2 teaspoon vanilla

Combine cocoa powder and hot water in small bowl; set aside.

Melt chocolate in large bowl in microwave in 30 second segments, stirring after each one. Cool slightly, 2 to 5 minutes.

Whip cream, sugar, vanilla and salt until soft peaks form.

Whisk cocoa powder mixture into melted chocolate until smooth. Fold whipped cream into chocolate mixture. Spoon mousse into spring form pan over cooled cake. Refrigerate cake at least 15 minutes while preparing top layer.

Top Layer:
3/4 teaspoon powdered gelatin
1 tablespoon water
6 ounces white chocolate chips
1-1/2 cups whipping cream
1 teaspoon vanilla
Shaved chocolate or cocoa powder (optional)

In small bowl, sprinkle gelatin over water; let stand at least 5 minutes.

Place white chocolate in medium bowl. Heat 1/2 cup cream in microwave, about 45 seconds, until hot but not boiling. Add gelatin mixture and stir until fully dissolved. Pour cream mixture over white chocolate and whisk until chocolate is melted and mixture is smooth, about 30 seconds. Cool to room temperature, stirring occasionally.

Whip remaining cup cream until soft peaks form. Fold whipped cream into white chocolate mixture. Spoon white chocolate mousse into pan over middle layer. Smooth top. Return cake to refrigerator and chill until set, at least 2 hours.

Garnish top of cake with chocolate curls or dust with cocoa. Run thin knife between cake and side of spring form pan; remove sides of pan. Cut into slices and serve.

Chocolate Scones

Place rack in center of oven and preheat to 375 degrees. Cover a baking sheet with parchment paper.

1/3 cup cream
1 large egg
1 teaspoon vanilla
1-3/4 cups flour
1/4 cup cocoa powder
1/2 cup sugar
2-1/2 teaspoons baking powder
1/8 teaspoon salt
1/3 cup butter, softened to room temperature
1/3 cup chocolate chips
1/3 cup white chocolate chips

In a small bowl, whisk together the cream, egg, and vanilla.

In a large bowl, mix flour, cocoa, sugar, baking powder and salt. Using a pastry blender, a big fork or a potato masher, blend butter into the flour mixture until it resembles coarse crumbs. Stir in the chocolate chips. Add the cream mixture and stir just until the dough sticks together.

Shape dough into a 7 inch circle, cut into eight wedges and place on the baking sheet.

Bake for 18-20 minutes or until firm around the edges but a little soft in the center. A toothpick inserted into the center of a scone will come out clean. Cool on a wire rack. Serve with whipped cream or chocolate syrup or whipped cream and chocolate syrup.

Suicide by Chocolate

With thanks to Kristy Jackson!

Preheat oven to 350 degrees. Grease a 9x13 inch pan.

Recipe of chocolate chip cookies (or cheat and use a tube of dough)
Recipe of brownies (or cheat and buy a family-size mix)
24 regular Oreo cookies
Recipe of chocolate fudge sauce (or cheat and buy a jar)
Recipe of caramel sauce (or cheat and buy a jar)
Vanilla bean ice cream

Spread cookie dough in bottom of pan. Layer with Oreos. Pour brownies over top. Bake at 350 degrees for 45 minutes.

Cool at least half an hour. Serve with ice cream, heated fudge syrup and heated caramel syrup.

Double Chocolate Cream Pie

1 cup sugar
1/4 cup cocoa
1/4 cup corn starch
Pinch of salt
3 cups milk or cream
3 egg yolks
1-1/2 teaspoons vanilla
1 cup chocolate chips
One 9" piecrust, baked & cooled
Sweetened whipped cream

In medium saucepan, combine sugar, cocoa, cornstarch and salt. Combine milk and egg yolks and whisk until well-blended. Add milk and egg mixture to the chocolate mixture, stirring until well blended. Cook mixture over medium heat until it thickens, stirring constantly (about 5 minutes). Remove from heat. Add vanilla and chocolate chips. Stir until completely blended. Pour into piecrust, allow to cool, cover and refrigerate until ready to serve. Top with whipped cream.

Sue Ross' Birthday Chocolate Cake

Heat oven to 400 degrees. Grease large pan (9x13 or 10x15). Dust with cocoa powder.

Put in mixing bowl:
2 cup sugar
2 cup flour

Put in sauce pan and bring to boil:
1 cup butter
1/4 cup cocoa
1 cup water

Pour heated mixture into flour mixture and blend well.

Add:
2 eggs
1/2 cup buttermilk
1 teaspoon soda
1 teaspoon vanilla

Pour mixture into pan and bake for 20 minutes.

When cake has been in oven ten minutes, put the following ingredients into sauce pan and bring to a boil:
1/2 cup butter
1/4 cup cocoa
1/3 cup milk

Chocolate Mousse Attack

Remove from heat and add:
1 box powdered sugar
1/2 cup chopped pecans
2 teaspoons vanilla

Pour over hot cake.

Perp Walk Brownies

Recipe of brownies (or cheat and buy a mix).
Make chocolate mousse (below).
Crumble half of brownies into a deep pan or a large bowl.
Pour mousse over brownies.
Crumble remaining brownies over top of mousse.
Top with whipped cream.
Sprinkle with miniature chocolate chips.
Sprinkle with chopped nuts.
Top with chocolate syrup and/or caramel syrup.

Chocolate Mousse

(Thanks to my Beta Sigma Phi sister, Julia Gibson, for sharing this recipe!)

6 oz. pkg. chocolate chips
1/2 lb. cream cheese
1 c. whipping cream
1/3 c. sugar
2 tsp. vanilla

Melt package of chocolate chips on low heat. Stir well then set on counter to cool. Combine cream cheese, sugar, salt, and vanilla with electric mixer. Add melted chocolate and stir until everything is blended and smooth again.

Chocolate Mousse Attack

Beat whipping cream till peaks form and then fold into chocolate mixture. Keep folding and blending softly until totally mixed.

About the Author:

I grew up in a small rural town in southeastern Oklahoma where our favorite entertainment on summer evenings was to sit outside under the stars and tell stories. When I went to bed at night, instead of a lullaby, I got a story. That could be due to the fact that everybody in my family has a singing voice like a bullfrog with laryngitis, but they sure could tell stories—ghost stories, funny stories, happy stories, scary stories.

For as long as I can remember I've been a storyteller. Thank goodness for computers so I can write down my stories. It's hard to make listeners sit still for the length of a book! Like my family's tales, my stories are funny, scary, dramatic, romantic, paranormal, magic.

Besides writing, my interests are reading, eating chocolate and riding my Harley.

Contact information is available on my website. I love to talk to readers! And writers. And riders. And computer programmers. Okay, I just plain love to talk!

http://www.sallyberneathy.com

Made in United States
North Haven, CT
01 February 2023

31943054R00143